#47

A Broken River Books Original
BROKEN RIVER BOOKS
Oklahoma City, OK

Front cover art by A.A. Medina
www.fabledbeastdesign.wordpress.com
Full wrap and interior layout by Kelby Losack
www.kelbylosack.com

ISBN: 978-1-940885-63-6

Printed in the USA.

Praise for Kelby Losack

"Kelby Losack is the Irvine Welsh of South Syrup City, the James Joyce of the Dirty Third Coast. His stories are full of heart, humor, grit, and brilliance. A legend in the making."

—Brian Allen Carr,
author of *Bad Foundations* and *Opioid, Indiana*

"Go home, folks, the king of hoodrat noir is here and the game is over."

—*PANK*

"...niche, artful writing that is meant for the thrill seekers, the existentially lonely and the emotionally violent."

—*Dead End Follies*

"If you aren't reading Kelby Losack's work, you're fucking up."

—Max Booth III,
author of *We Need to Do Something*

STORY CREDITS

"Chicken and Waffles" appeared in *The Broken River Writers' Collective*; a completely different story with the title "Daddy's In a Snuff Film" appeared in *Lost Films*, this new version appeared in *Rare Candy*; "God Is Wearing Black" appeared in *Apocalypse Confidential*; a much shorter version of "The Adventures of Naked Man" appeared in *555 Vol. 3: Questions & Cancers*; "The Snowy Graves of Camp Bragg" appeared in *Bleak Friday*; "The Future" appeared in *Dark Moon Digest #27*; "Gas Tank" appeared in *Red Fez*; "Flesh and Blood" appeared in *Gaia: Shadow & Breath*; *Hurricane Season* was originally published as a standalone limited print run book; "Eden's Bastards" appeared in *Forever Magazine*; "Perro," "Cambion," and "Jellyfish In Geometry" are original publications to this collection.

CONTENTS

for everyone praying ya boy stays alive and out the pen

CHICKEN AND WAFFLES

They got this deal at Waffle King where if you get their logo permanently inked in your skin, you can go in and cop a free combo meal as much as once a week. The tattoo can be any size, on any part of your body. You ain't gotta go putting that shit on your temple, too big for a band-aid or the brim of a hat to cover, you know, in the event you chew your homie's face off and gotta keep it lowkey for a minute.

You ain't gotta go all Kennedy Wilder for the free meals, is what I'm saying. All you gotta do is show that fool's mugshot to a tattoo artist or your tweaker cousin—the one who's got that eBay rig and just got laid off from the plant—and you can point to the dripping waffle-patterned crown cocked sideways over Kennedy's right eyebrow and say, "That's what I want. But smaller. And not on my damn head, you feel me. Maybe on my ankle or something."

Then you'd have to do some stretching while making your way up to the register, 'cause once it's your turn to order, you'll have to swing your leg up onto the counter to redeem the branded flesh, still swollen and crusty and shimmering in A&D ointment, it's so fresh. Or you could get it on your wrist, I mean, yeah. Some folks do that, so it's small enough to cover with a watch or bracelet. Or, shit, if you really want to keep it lowkey outside of these transactions, there's no fine print that says flashing or mooning the clerk would nullify the value of the tattoo, you feel me.

They've seen it all at Waffle King.

Since Kennedy Wilder first showed up with the right side of his head all puffy and red, all the way up until he got arrested in the parking lot, they'd seen old boy in that joint once a week for his free chicken and waffles. He ain't ever switched it up, either; it's chicken and waffles every time. He'd stroll up to the counter with his shoulders arched back, hands drumming on his flat stomach, and whoever was working register would see that grayscale waffle crown etched behind a curtain of bleached blond curls and they'd already know what to punch into the queue: a number three combo with a pink lemonade.

Then Kennedy would stand there and wait, entranced by the glowing specter of those syrup-smothered, Cajun-battered breasts atop a buttermilk stack orbiting his head. This last time he popped in to redeem the tattoo was no different, except for the crimson butterfly wings painted across his lips, Shiloh's blood still dripping from his chin and eyelashes. That and the fact he was naked down to his Jordans. But the only thing on old boy's mind in that moment—besides the number three combo—was the chick working register's nameplate. He said her name three times to himself while imagining holding his own daughter, who was due to drop any day now.

Chloe, Chloe, Chloe.

The name was a solid maybe.

Chloe had punched in the order without even thinking bout it. Pure force of habit. Maybe one of the slack-jawed fry cooks would snap out of it enough to call the cops. Or maybe one of the patrons who'd fled screaming had already beaten them to it.

Meantime, old boy stands there waiting on his last free meal, his eyes all pupils as he absently sucks the blood off his bottom lip, his mind somewhere between his daughter's name and the blend of sweet and spicy that's got him salivating with that dumb, distant grin on his mug, the rest of his mind long gone.

Zombie.

Layla had told him the shit was going to rot his brain. "It says right there on the package," what she told him, pointing at the holographic blue foil amidst the Big Swig fountain drinks and the loose change being counted out. "Do not eat," she said, reading off the label.

The label also said it was plant food, but everybody—Layla, too—knew better than that. The shit in the shiny foil wrapper looking like Pokémon cards was called ZOOM, all caps. Kennedy had pointed it out at random behind the glass at the Texaco station.

What he could tell, there didn't seem to be a difference between the brands. Cloud 9, Ocean Wave, White Lightning—it all hit the same.

Kennedy's devil-horned clone appeared on his shoulder to remind him why he fucked with the shit. "You can fly through a week in a day off this shit right here," the imp said. "Feel the rhythm of your heart as it pumps blood through your dick and everything in the world slows down except for you. You can witness the kaleidoscopic dance of chemical compounds within grains of sugar. You can feel the electric currents that emanate off every living being." The imp leaned against Kennedy's neck and whispered up into his ear, "Lowkey, you just walking around with your eyes open. This shit will make you feel *alive*."

Layla's voice was coming in muffled as if underwater. Kennedy's shoulder devil went on, "And I know how you be dozing behind the wheel coming off of them shutdowns at the plant. Shit ain't safe, big dawg. You need something to wake your ass up and make it home in one piece. It ain't like you ever gonna sleep during the day. Hell nah, you got music to make." The imp who looked just like old boy leaned back on his palms and kicked his feet off the edge of Kennedy's shoulder. "Plus," he said, "the shit is synthetic. A drug test will ding you on amphetamines, but cathinone? Fuck you know bout the Ugandan euphoria plant? Nothing. Don't nobody know bout that shit. So you straight."

The clerk wore a red hijab and an oversized Rockets jersey. She said, "Is this going to be all?"

The devil in his ear threw Kennedy off his count. He palmed the pile of coins and crumpled bills across the chipped laminate countertop and nodded at the '94 Taurus parked out at the pump. Said, "Lemme get whatever's left on three."

The clerk rang up the Big Swigs and the designer speed dressed as plant food. Kennedy asked her name. She said, "Fatima."

Kennedy glanced at Layla. She stood with her arms crossed over the bump stretching her shirt tight. She shook her head slowly.

Fatima said, "You have $3.37 on pump three."

It was enough to make it down to Surfside. They could worry bout how to make it home once they got there.

It was 2012 and the world was finna end and Kennedy and Layla were heading down to the beach, tryna come up with a name for the baby girl in Layla's belly.

They passed by a priest throwing up a new message on his church's marquee.

Kennedy said, "What about Grace?"

They passed by a sex shop advertising a new porn star-modeled pocket pussy.

Layla said, "What about Alexis?"

Palm trees and miles of labyrinthine steel stole the scenery for the rest of the ride down to the gulf. The chemical plant was seven thousand acres of pipes that snaked between burning towers and tanks the size of skyscrapers. In a ditch off the side of the highway, a flock of gulls cawed and pecked at a gutted gar that'd been tossed from a fisherman's truck.

Kennedy drove onto the crowded free beach, where one long stretch of tents and tailgates faced the choppy mud-colored waves. He found a gap between a couple F-150s to park the Taurus. Said a silent prayer that he wouldn't have to beg for a tow when it came time to leave.

Kennedy and Layla kicked their shoes off in the floorboard and walked hand-in-hand into the tide, ankles deep, just to where they could feel the sand steady slipping away beneath their feet. Kennedy pulled out his phone to take pictures of Layla caressing her swollen belly and gazing off into the distance, at barges and offshore oil rigs just outside of frame. He wrapped his arms around her waist from behind and held the phone up against the sun to snap a selfie of them both smiling down at her belly.

Waves crashed and gulls cawed overhead while a chaotic clash of tejano, chopped-and-screwed, and pop country blasted from pill-shaped speakers. The couple walked up and down the beach plucking shells from the sand. They filled their pockets with sundials and cowries and those spiky drill-shaped conches, whatever you call those. They'd been looking for a place to move in together, some place with a room for the baby. Layla would incorporate the shells somehow in decorating the nursery.

They kicked at crushed beer cans and stepped over pulsating man-o'-wars. Kennedy found a sand dollar next to a hollow .223 cartridge. He pocketed both.

The inside of the car and the clothes they wore would have that coconut and sulfur beach smell for days. Back on the road, Layla said, "So you're not even kinda nervous?"

And Kennedy grinned, said, "Fuck I gotta be nervous for? I'm finna have two reasons to keep on living."

Part two, Kennedy had been splitting rent on a shotgun duplex with this juggalo named Shiloh. That was old boy's gummer name, at least. Whenever he was wearing the clown paint and rapping bout unrequited love for dead hoes, he was Hatchet Samurai.

They'd fucked with each other since middle school and shared dreams of leaving the Third Coast since before they had jobs. Spent most their off time tryna get the music shit to pop off. Kennedy used to fuck around on guitar all through high school, but got into making beats when he and Shiloh moved in together.

Now Kennedy was moving out. He went through the house with a box on his hip, filling it up with manga, lighters, shuriken he'd ordered off the internet, dinner plates he'd inherited from grandma. When the box became too stuffed to close, he carried it out to the Taurus and shoved it in the backseat along with the MIDIs, drum machines, and mixing boards, then he grabbed another box from next to the trash cans and repeated the process. Ended up with three overflowing boxes and a backpack full of clothes.

Shiloh sat on the stoop during all this, hissing and groaning while Fingers twisted his hair into box braids. Fingers was their neighbor from the other side of the duplex. She kept telling Shiloh to sit still and quit being a baby, laughing bout his tender white boy scalp.

They called her Fingers 'cause she had one arm. Her real name was Gertrude. Kennedy wasn't sure which was worse, but neither went on the list of potential names for his daughter.

In the men's room at Club VIP, at two in the afternoon on a Thursday, Kennedy ripped the foil off a pack of Vanilla Sky and sniffed that shit off the stainless steel rim of the sink. The bath salts hotwired his brain and lit his insides on fire and after a minute, he felt invincible. He sent a text to Layla: *what about Sky?*

He and Shiloh would be playing a set there at the club the following night. They were meeting the owner to go over the sound system and shit, but mostly, Shiloh just wanted to get day drunk and fuck the bartender in the handicap stall.

Kennedy shadowboxed himself in the mirror and bled from his nose. Louder than necessary, he said, "Aye, what's your name?"

The bartender told him one syllable at a time, in sync with getting her cheeks clapped.

"*Is-a-bell-a.*"

Shiloh said, "Bro, shut the fuck up."

Kennedy left them in the bathroom to finish doing their thing. He sent another text to Layla.

Night before the show, Kennedy was part of a shutdown crew in block D. The night's objective was to get a scaffold erected so they could start breaking down a benzene pipeline that'd been tagged and killed. This the kinda job that if it wasn't for the auditors and his foreman on his dick bout doing overhead work without a harness, Kennedy could have it done all by himself in thirty minutes.

It's just poles sliding into other poles.

Lock pins and ladders.

Toe boards and cross bracing.

Only leftovers he'd get flagged for would be the guard rails, but come on, how much protection you need to unbolt a couple pipes from each other? By the time the whole thing's up, you're lying flat beneath the pipes you're working with, the little grip teeth of the metal planks digging into your back. Couldn't fall off if you wanted to, probably. But you also shouldn't be building the scaffold that tall because you shouldn't be lying underneath the pipes you're uncoupling, so Kennedy was put on fire watch duty down on the ground.

He'd snorted some bath salts off the dash of the work truck and now his insides were burning up. He leaned against an I-beam and rode out the shift with his heart beating in his teeth, eyeballs rattling in his skull, knowing full well he could throw that fucking scaffold up in thirty seconds, tops.

Kennedy spent that night in bed with Layla in their new apartment. She told him when he woke drenched in sweat that he'd been growling in his sleep.

"You were scaring me," is what she said, and he pouted his lips and bulged his eyes like a mangy mongrel puppy, and he said, "You ain't gotta be scared, babe," and he kissed her neck until she shoved him off for biting too hard.

This is the last day they spent together without ballistic glass between them. They ate gas station tacos and shifted the baby crib around the nursery. Decided it fit best caddy-corner against the wall opposite the window. They kept the TV on some game show channel, listening for a name to jump out at them, but none did. They rolled down to Club VIP with the windows down 'cause the A/C was busted. Something had baby girl bouncing around in her momma's belly. Maybe the wind, maybe Lil Ugly Mane's "Throw Dem Gunz" bumping on max to drown out the wind. Kennedy drove with one hand on the wheel and one hand against his daughter's kicks.

Emma, Jasmine, Brooke.

Somewhere in the back of Kennedy's mind, the part of his brain that hadn't gone zombie yet, he considered the names of the chicks staring at him with trembling hands cupped over their mouths.

Crowds at these local shows were always people you'd known since grade school. If Kennedy and Layla were having a boy, there'd be four different names to consider between the dudes tugging at old boy's arms and hair—anywhere they could grab tryna yank him off of Shiloh.

Last time he did bath salts, instead of snorting the shit, Kennedy took a fistful of the ivory crystals and funneled them into his mouth like they were sunflower seeds. This was during sound check, while old boy was uncoiling cables to run from the drum machine through the interface, from his laptop to the mixing board, from there to the house speakers. Whole time, Shiloh paced the short plywood stage shouting *whoop, whoop* in different octaves into the mic.

"*Whoop, whoop*—cut that echo—*whoop, whoop*—turn me up, dawg—*whoop, whoop*—what's going on with this other speaker—*WHOOP, WHOOP*—okay, okay, turn it down, yo."

He was in full Hatchet Samurai mode. Box braids looking tight, grease-painted clown face, cubic zirconia Cuban links glistening against his stick-and-poke tatted chest, oversize camo jacket swallowing his shirtless skinny frame.

Last remnants of golden daylight still spilled through the windows on the face of the club. Dust motes sparkling like a galaxy of filth above the sticky concrete dance floor. There might have been a dozen people including them and the bartenders, but the *whoop, whoop* shouted back at him from the bar got Shiloh hyped to jump in. He smooched Kennedy on the forehead, right between old boy's black hole pupils, and said, "Lesgo, baby boy."

Layla was kicked back sipping on a virgin daquiri in the booth beside the stage. Little momma smiled at old boy and he winked at her and felt his heart punch his ribcage.

He blacked out sometime between the beat drop on "Cadaver Ho" and the hook on "Sippin' Bleach."

If you were one of the handful of sweaty bodies spilling plastic cups of Hennessy in the world's smallest mosh pit, the way you'd say it went down is all of a sudden, the DJ with the Waffle King logo tatted on his forehead started fanning himself with his shirt and growling like maybe he was dry retching, or like he was possessed by a demon or some shit, then he peeled his shirt off and slipped out of his basketball shorts and his boxers before knocking all his equipment to the ground and tackling the juggalo from behind. And it'd take a minute to register what was going down with the screaming and the gurgling and the red spilling across the floor, flowing towards your sneakers, like is this really happening?

Pregnant chick in the booth near the stage had gone catatonic and pale and at some point you snapped out of the dream and you were either screaming now yourself or taking your phone out, struggling between pressing the camera icon and dialing 911. Or you were one of the dudes tryna yank the naked psycho off the juggalo, whose gurgling screams had gone silent, and when the psycho was finally ripped away from the body on the ground, you could see why.

From his paint-flecked scalp to his lower jaw, Shiloh's face was a crater of glistening meat.

The zombie spit a wad of chewed flesh on the dance floor and broke out of the four-man armbar and made a mad dash toward the door. If you were the bartender with the crew cut and gorilla arms, you probably felt pretty brave there for the couple seconds you stood in the charging zombie's way, but locking eyes with him, seeing all that blood dripping from his nose to his chin, from his chest to his dick—nobody thinks less of you for crouching out the way like you did and letting old boy go.

And if you were Kennedy Wilder, at some point in your naked sprint down Skinner Street onto Gulf Boulevard, your breathing slowed and your pupils shrank and some part of your consciousness crawled up out the pit it'd been tossed in and all you could think about as you stood in the neon yellow glow of the Waffle King sign was how you'd yet to redeem your free combo meal this week.

Chloe's hands shook as she carried the paper-lined basket of chicken and waffles to the vinyl booth you'd claimed by the window. You were sipping a pink lemonade, watching the red and blue lights grow brighter out in the parking lot. You thanked Chloe when she nearly dropped your food all over the table. Another drop of red collected in your eyelashes and you squinted, took another napkin from the silver casket on the table. Wiped your face. You wadded up the bloody napkin and tossed it in a pile that was already stacked higher than your waffles.

You were unwrapping your silverware when the cops came in with their hands on their hips, yelling at you to get on the ground.

"On the fucking ground, *now!*"

You're not sure why you complied so easily. You did nothing wrong. You were just tryna enjoy the sweet and spicy combo of some Cajun fried chicken and some syrup-drenched waffles. Maybe it was how all this still felt like a dream you'd wake up from any moment now. Yeah, you were floating too far outside your body for this to be real. And how come you're buck-ass naked? The fuck? Whose blood is that?

The cold steel wrapping around your wrists brought you halfway back. Your head smacking the roof of the squad car brought you the rest of the way. Hands stuck between your back and the hot leather seats, you couldn't wipe the red dripping from your eyelashes. You mumbled something and the cops up front said you ain't gotta say a word. They said please, for the love of god, don't. They told you to shut the fuck up.

But you finally had it. Couldn't stop saying it.

The blood had pooled in your eyes and you couldn't blink it away. Vision gone completely red.

"Ruby, Ruby, Ruby."

You said it over and over again until the cop who said to shut the fuck up punched the ceiling and screamed.

"The fuck are you saying?!"

And you said it again, would go on saying it forever, while airplaning spoonfuls of mashed avocado into her toothless mouth, while holding onto the seat of her bike as she pedaled for the first time without training wheels, while walking her down the aisle tryna swallow the knot in your throat.

"Ruby," you said. "That's my daughter's name."

Daddy's In a Snuff Film

I'ma tell this story backwards so it has a happy ending. Thought about leaving no letter at first, just to be extra sure you grow up wanting to be nothing like your old man. Lowkey, though, the best way to be sure you hate me forever is to just tell you everything. Tryna imagine how old you might be when you find this. I'ma fold this letter up into a little square just big enough to write "I love you" on one side and "I'm sorry" on the other, then I'll slip it inside your piggy bank. If all goes down the way it should, and if bad luck ain't genetic, you won't have to go breaking that open for a hot minute. Right now, you're rolling across the living room floor from one end of the rug to the other, back and forth, your slobber-soaked fingers collecting lint and dirt and I'm telling you "no no no, quit shoving your dirty fists in your mouth," but you're cutting teeth, you ain't gon listen to me. You just gazed up at me with those big hazel eyes that take up half your cute little head and the way you just cooed and chuckled will forever be the way I know the sound of your voice.

I love you, and I'm sorry.

Here's how our last night together is finna go down: I'll take you down to the beach and we'll walk together through the tide, your hands wrapped around my index fingers while I'm hunched over, puppeteering you since you ain't walking on your own yet, and you'll giggle at the feel of the slick sand and the seafoam bubbling over your feet and I'll take pictures on my phone to send to your mom. The sun's been setting closer to eight lately, so the sky will be all pink and purple, or maybe red—I don't really know how the sun decides what colors to set in, but the pictures will be pretty. Then I'll find a crab shell and hold it up to your ear and say, "hear that? It's the sound of ghost whispers. It's daddy saying he loves you." You won't remember this, but maybe this shell is still hanging around somewhere, lost in a drawer or a shoebox of random baby shit. Maybe you can still pick it up and hear me.

I love you, and I'm sorry.

After the beach, you'll be hungry, because you're always hungry, so I'll prop your bottle up with a blanket across your chest and you'll fall asleep eating in your stroller on the walk home. It's a three-mile walk, bout an hour to go under the piss jar-colored light of street lamps and the flames blowing out the tops of the burn towers. This would be my chance to think twice about everything, if I had any better ideas.

Fucked up part is I can't even kill myself the old fashioned way, since you gotta pay for life insurance to have it.

Learn from daddy's mistakes: take out a life insurance policy. Better yet, aspire to be more valuable to your loved ones while you're still breathing.

Later on, when your mom gets home, she'll unwind on the front porch with a coffee and a cigarette. She'll swat at june bugs and moths flying kamikaze halos round her head and she'll play a puzzle game on her phone. Then she'll come inside and shower off all the glitter clinging to her face, her shoulders, her thighs, her C-section scar. Flakes of silver and gold that don't make it down the drain become stuck in the no-slip ridges at the base of the tub; this leftover glitter forming constellations for you to float across when you pretend to be an astronaut during bath time.

You remember doing that?

When she gets out of the shower, your mom will slide up next to where me and you are crashed out on the couch. I'll be sitting there with surrendered arms at my sides, snoring at the ceiling with you sideways across my lap, stirring and stretching from a Statue of Liberty pose into a baby crucifix, a stream of drool running cross your cheek, into your ear. She'll gently lift you from my lap and carry you to your crib and she'll part your curly hair to kiss your forehead. She'll whisper wishes of sweet dreams into your ear and she'll mean it because she won't know what happens next.

When I bought the chainsaw, I meant to make us some money with it, just not in the way you probably know by now. Your old man never wanted to be a star. Just wanted your mom to worry less, wanted you to have an easier go of things.

One thing I'll say is learn some type of trade, something people don't usually think they can do themselves, like plumbing. Or HVAC. Summertime spells death to air conditioners all over Texas—that's called job security. Better yet, you know the median salary of an electrician in this state? You can be an uneducated felon with swollen pockets if you're the one swapping knob-and-tube out for Romex in these old-ass houses folks cop on the low. Just don't be a carpenter like your old man. By the time you're grown, homes will be metal-framed concrete atrocities furnished in plastic, cabinets built out of some Dow-trademarked chemical compound that will be the source of a class-action lawsuit for causing cancer in fifty years. If I'd have learned a trade in anything outside of lumber, well.

Maybe I'd be saying all this to your face.

There's only so many "nevermind"s and "lemme save a bit"s you can take before you go from quoting someone on a beach house balcony to standing in line at the pawn shop—tool box in one hand, shotgun in the other. Repeat until you're down to a screwdriver on top of the fridge and a Glock under the driver's seat and you're still choosing the lights over the phones come first of the month.

Saying shit like, "Kids don't even remember their first birthdays."

I love you, and I'm sorry.

Wasn't even that your old man was stubbornly tryna get it the honest way. Your mom had been tryna talk me out the game for a minute before you came along as the final ultimatum.

"Us or the pills."

It was an easy choice until the ramen joint got shut down for gutting pigs right there in the alleyway, and your mom went from making dogshit per hour serving noodles to dogshit per hour sliding down a pole. Whole time, your old man walking around with a pocket full of "nevermind"s and stolen packets of baby formula, thinking *if she gon get it by any means, so am I.*

Problem with selling pills is you gotta have pills to sell, so you gotta know niggas with pills. In the timespan you went from two solid lines on a stick to a screaming little creature with your mother's eyes and lips, all the plugs I used to know got themselves locked up or buried. Dead end. So I quickly learned how big a plasma needle is (bigger than my veins, which is probably why they blew out both arms and sent me home with a thirty-five dollar courtesy comp and cotton balls tied to the crooks of my elbows). Then I learned any app that has you drive around picking up groceries for people costs you half what you make in gas. I learned that being a test dummy for a new migraine medication will score you fifty bucks plus tinnitus and a migraine. I learned you can cram all this bullshit into a week while waiting on a potential client to hit you back with a "nevermind" on building their bathroom vanity and you'll end up with a whole third of what you need for groceries and shit.

Just now, you crawled over fussing to be picked up and so I picked you up and you vomited on my lap. I made you a bottle and changed your diaper and now you're rubbing your belly with one hand and holding the bottle with the other and you're grinning up at me from where I laid you down on the couch and there's streams of formula running out both corners of your mouth, dripping down your chin. You're making it hard to see this through.

I keep reminding myself how many times this year I've held your mom in fits of panic, how many times she's shoved me off and wished I was someone who knew how to take care of the two of you, how many times she's had to dance through a sinus infection or a toothache just so at least one of us is making some bread.

This would be so much easier if you'd please stop smiling and start hating me already.

You want to know some behind-the-scenes shit?

The chainsaw wasn't in the script. I haven't actually seen the script, if there is one, but I know the premise, and I know the director got the idea to use the chainsaw when I told him bout how I'd been going door to door with this chainsaw offering to cut down trees.

My pitch would go like this: knock on the door, stand there like a sweaty idiot with a chainsaw, move on when no one answers, then when someone finally does answer, say, "aye bro/excuse me ma'am, could I cut down this tree for you here? This one out near the driveway that look like it's ready to fall over and total that Sonata you got there?" Then I'd wink and say, "Unless that's what you praying for—I get it, why you think I'm out here with a chainsaw?—but anyway, check this out," then I'd go and push on the tree and go, "see, I ain't even gon need the saw for much besides chopping it up for the trash man, this bitch finna fall over on its own. So what you think, sixty bucks and I'll take care of this for you right now." And they'd say they ain't got the money, but they'd think about it and could I leave a card or my number, and they'd be saying this just to get rid of me, I know, 'cause they'd be shifting their weight from one foot to the other, taking their hands in and out of their pockets like they knew they were finna get robbed by a skinny peckerwood with a chainsaw. So I'd say, "How bout twenty bucks? Please. I got a kid to feed." And they'd say no. They'd say please leave before they call the cops. And I'd take off down the road and round the block and start knocking on doors again, the sweat hiding the tears.

If I hadn't shared that story with the director, who knows what he'd be taking your daddy's head off with. Maybe a samurai sword. That would have been crazy.

It wasn't tree-cutting that brought me to the director's door, though. The Budget Motel off 288 going down to Freeport doesn't even have any trees around.

Nah, I ain't go down there with the chainsaw, I went down with the Glock. Rolled up splashing through the potholes in the parking lot and hopped out too quick to lose the nerve. Hands in the pockets of my Carhartt, ready to pull that thing out soon as the chump in Room 626 opens the door, ready to up that barrel in his eye socket and shove him back into the room to kick the door closed, tell him to come off it, all of it, whatever he's got, think I'm playin, nigga, try me.

What fucked the plan up was assuming he'd just open the door for anyone. Of course he'd check through the peephole, hoping to see lil shorty from the pictures I posted on this local hookup subreddit, and when instead he sees this sketchy 'wood with his hands stuffed in jacket pockets, he'd open up just a crack—chain lock still in the slide—and he'd up his own piece at your daddy's torso, ready to blow the ramen noodles out his guts.

Your daddy would say, "Shit." He'd turn grey while his heart pounded in his skull and he'd fight to stay standing on gelatin legs.

The director, though, as if he was half-expecting to get someone like me, he'd say, "Come inside, son. I think we can help each other."

I don't know the casting process of other snuff film stars, but people get discovered in crazier places, probably.

I don't know.

Probably not.

I hope to god you ain't seen this movie.

Supposed to be one of those slow-burn psychological joints, shot POV style through the eyes of a killer.

But you wouldn't know he was a killer for most of the movie, 'cause I guess he's not, at least not at first.

The director said he's got all the footage leading up to the climax.

Shots of the chemical plant silhouetted against a blood red sunset.

A blue crab dragging a used condom over balled-up fast food wrappers on the beach.

Scenes of the not-yet-killer white-knuckling a sink or a steering wheel while the camera—representing his vision—wobbles and warps while the film's droning score of buzzing and shrieking climbs to an ear-piercing crescendo. You know, to give the vibe of going crazy or whatever. The director said it'll come together in the editing.

Sounds like a movie bout nothing with a random murder at the end. All I know is I got an address to a barn way the fuck out near Matagorda, off 35 somewhere outside Bay City, and I can't forget to bring the chainsaw. That's the money shot, the viral moment. You want to know some more behind-the-scenes magic? The director said he'll fix your daddy up with some fenty, so I won't be feeling it too-too bad when all those spinning teeth on the chain start biting at my neck. The most authentic arterial spray ever caught on camera, that's what the director's going for. I'll be floating on a black cloud somewhere high above my own body before the saw cuts through the neck bone.

I didn't even need to know all this. I was in when the director said it'd be fifty racks paid out as an anonymous donation soon as we wrapped. He already had the donation page made and ready to go. Had me input my bank routing number to receive the posthumous funds. So while he was going on bout how this was finna put him in the ranks of those Italian niggas who cut up real life turtles on screen, all I was thinking bout was what you and your mom could do with fifty Gs.

I love you, and I'm sorry.

Lupe, the old lady next door, says we've been hit with *el mal de ojo*, the evil eye. That's why we've been so unlucky. That's why the hurricane dropped that tree onto your mom's car same time we were cutting back on insurance payments. That's why the freeze came same week we brought you home from the hospital. Talmbout five days of no power with a six-pound newborn. Extension cords running out the window to the generator, plugged in to the heat lamp clamped to your bassinet, where we swaddled you with the thickest blankets and took turns drying your tears so your face wouldn't freeze.

If life flashes before your eyes at the end like people say, I hope mine plays in rewind and stops at when I met your mom, my first job out the pen washing dishes at the noodle shop, taking up smoking just to bum cigarettes and flirt on our breaks. But first, let it play through the first time you lifted yourself up on hands and knees to crawl across the living room, a moment of pride and joy for the three of us, but also of fear for your mom and me at all the shit you were finna get into now that you were mobile. Rewind to late nights stripping you down and holding you in front of the fridge, tryna lower your temperature while you wailed at the pain of cutting your first tooth. Rewind to when the doctor said you had the umbilical cord wrapped around your neck and we had to move quick, had to wheel your mom down the hall to a room big enough to pitch a tent over her body up to her neck, a room big enough for all the nurses running around with whirring tools and pipe clamps and napkins soaked in blood to not trip over each other, a room I stood outside of dressed in the scrubs they threw at me, ready to bust in if they didn't come grab me soon and say I could come run my finger down your mom's cheek, tell her it'd all be okay, and shed more than a couple tears when it turned out

I wasn't lying to her. Rewind to the first time I heard your voice, the first time you opened up your lungs and screamed to tell us you were here, you were alive.

Now fast forward back to our last night together. After your mom lays you down in your crib and kisses your forehead, whispers wishes of sweet dreams in your ear, she'll come back to the couch and rub my chest to wake me up. She'll sit in my lap and wrap her arms around my neck and ask how the day went, she'll say the pictures we took at the beach were adorable as hell, she'll pull me towards the bedroom and act like she's not about to fall asleep as soon as her head touches the pillow.

It'll be five in the morning. I'll be dressed already, chainsaw the only thing to grab on my way out.

Before slipping out, I'll leave a separate letter just for your mom on her nightstand.

It will simply say I love you, and I'm sorry.

PERRO

They found the bitch at the corner of Overland and Tornillo. Caught her in the headlights, her shadow stretching up and over a derailed boxcar. She was limping along the trainyard fence in search of a hole big enough to slip through. Felipe slowed the Bronco to a crawl and Benicio hopped out and scooped her up from behind. Carried her back to the truck with all three legs pointing forward. He dropped the bitch in the floorboard and climbed in the passenger seat and slammed the door shut. Felipe busted a 'U' and the Bronco fishtailed a few feet, rocking their bodies against each other.

"Been having nightmares of dogs," Benicio said. "Packs of them, chasing me across the desert, eating me alive."

Felipe fidgeted with the radio. Commercials in English, commercials in Spanish, Miley Cyrus. The CD player only worked when they hit a pothole at the right speed. Felipe settled on a tejano station and resisted the urge to crank the volume higher than four.

"Some nights," Benicio said, "I dream I *am* a dog. Those are the worst, because I'm still myself, but as a dog. And so I know what I know, and I know I'll never get away."

They kept to neighborhood roads. San Antonio to Noble and then north on Cotton under the overpass. Sagging fences, scalped lawns, blue tarps on roofs.

Felipe said nothing for a solid minute. Then he threw his head back and howled. He punched the ceiling and lurched forward over the steering wheel, wheezing with a laughter so strong it choked him and his face went red. He wiped tears from his eyes and when he caught his breath, he said to Benicio, "You should drink more. I see nothing when I sleep."

The bitch lay her head in Benicio's lap. She was an Oreo-colored Chamuco with a railroad of staples up and down her belly. She'd chewed through the rope and jumped out the busted window of the turtle shell just this side of Paso del Norte, where they'd picked her up off the family paid to bring her through. Felipe Hernandez and Benicio Verdugo had spent all day hunting up and down the canal, looking in drainage ditches and behind dumpsters and under parked cars, all places the bitch took to hiding, just not in the order they'd looked.

Now it was over. The bitch was caught, and she was tired.

Felipe said, "Quit petting it," and Benicio dropped his hand to his side.

Benicio Verdugo scrubbed the gut crumbs out from under his fingernails with a baby toothbrush. Sink bowl a mess with what looked like bloody granules of sand. Water running hot enough to fog up the bathroom. Felipe Hernandez was outside lying under the Bronco, taping torpedoes of vacuum-sealed dope up inside the oil pan. He'd grabbed the new one they'd cut out of the three-legged runaway, plus seven more kilos from behind a removable piece of drywall under the kitchen sink. Decided to stuff the other two keys he should have been carrying in the couch cushions.

He'd asked Verdugo if he wanted him to take care of the trash and Verdugo had said, "I'll handle it," standing there with his hands held under the faucet turned to scalding hot, fingers twitching, palms wilting raw pink, and last thing Hernandez said to him before dipping out of the city was, "It's bagged up in the shed."

What that meant was, *hit the dumpster behind Tractor Supply or Sonic at 3am.* Or, *toss it in the river.* Or, *drive real fast down I-10 with the tailgate off.*

Instead, when Verdugo went out to the shed and hefted the black trash bag over his shoulder, he also grabbed a shovel. Then he found a spot in the patchwork yard of yellow grass and dirt that hadn't been dug out yet.

He said an apology and a prayer, but after drinking enough to black out, Benicio Verdugo still dreamed of being chased through the desert by a horde of growling, drooling mongrels.

Felipe tried to give him a heads up, but Benicio kept declining the unknown Arizona numbers. Benicio ignored all numbers, for that matter. He found a stray mutt limping with its head low and carried it home. Brushed the knots out of its fur. Bathed it. Fed it chicken and beer. He was petting the sleeping mutt in his lap and imagining patterns in the ceiling texture—dragons and demons and dogs—when he was too late noticing the shadows through the curtains.

They kicked in the front and back doors and tossed a flashbang through the kitchen window and in the fever dream white, muffled underwater with an echoing latency, Verdugo heard the barking, then the gunshot, then nothing besides the ringing in his ears.

No words could be heard, but his lips moved in the shape of a prayer.

He'd catch the broadcasts in prison—feral dogs hunting down mules from Cuidad to El Paso, sometimes solo, sometimes in packs a dozen large—and he'd swear he'd seen it all before through a different set of eyes. Could taste the blood in his mouth. Tongued the phantom flesh stuck between his incisors.

Benicio Verdugo was one of a dozen inmates cooked alive in their cells that summer. Died facedown on the concrete in a pool of sweat, same dream of a mongrel pack in the desert, only this time they were leading instead of chasing him.

On the bank of the Rio Grande, a pregnant pitbull collapses and spills her pups into the clay. The runt is an Oreo-colored bitch born with three legs. The bitch whimpers and crawls blindly through the muck to nurse from her mother, nightmares of running through the desert fading with each sip of warm milk.

GOD IS WEARING BLACK

Last time I saw Miles was just before he went to prison for tryna kill his stepdad. I wasn't there when it went down and by the time the story floated my way, it's like—take it with a grain of salt, right? Except everybody knows Miles is crazy, so when I was told he burned the old man's face off for saying something bout Miles's daughter pronouncing her *R*s funny, I thought *bet, that sounds like Miles.*

So his daughter—she gotta be five, maybe six—she's telling her daddy what kinda rice she wants to go with the fajitas he's whipping up, and her granddaddy—Miles's stepdad—chuckles and mimics the way she says it.

"Wice."

Just a cute little kid thing, you know.

But this is coming from the man who felt the best discipline for backtalk from a teenage stepson was a belt across the mouth, so yeah, we all know grandparents are different with their grandkids, but still. Miles takes the mimicking some type of way. Grabs the old man by the back of the neck and shoves his face into the skillet that's over the burner. So his face is sizzling and popping in steak grease—he's screaming and flailing and Miles's mom is tryna get her boy off her man before he melts his face down to the bone—and you gotta imagine baby girl is losing her shit, if not sitting there quietly traumatized.

But Miles wasn't tryna kill nobody last time I saw him.

He didn't even have a skillet.

How I know Miles is he was married to my cousin Tonya for a minute. She met him at a house party his shitty band was playing at and a couple months later, they couldn't afford a Plan B. Decided "fuck it, this is us now." Tonya didn't slow down with the XOs, though, which is maybe how come their daughter was born with a heart arrhythmia and how come she says her *R*s like *W*s.

But who am I to judge.

I was the one feeding her habit at least half the time.

That's the reason all three of us fucked with each other like we did, really, was the XOs. Miles and his shitty band would attract a good-enough number of dead-eyed customers to the bars they played at, so I could just do my thing in the parking lot and chill. Easy money. The band, though—Sons of Paimon—they really did suck, I ain't gon lie to you. Miles was the singer. He did a lot of that screaming shit. This one time, though, they played a cover of "Soldier Side" by System of a Down. Go look that up and play that joint, I'll be done with the story before it's over. But this the only song that nigga could sing well, and it ain't like he was singing on key. He absolutely was not. The Sons of Paimon butchered this shit. Screeching the wrong notes on the guitar riff, drums and bass all out of rhythm with each other. And like I said, Miles can't carry a note to save his life, but when he sang this song, it was coming from somewhere else. Like the him that wasn't haunted by some demon was singing from somewhere deep inside. He's at the edge of the stage, leaning out over the dozen people gathered there washing their XOs down with beer and his eyes are bugging out his head and he's got this crazy Joker smile. This is when his teeth were all crooked and sharp, too, before they got blasted out his mouth and he had them replaced with perfect fakes. Real devilish.

To this day when I hear this song, I leave my body for a minute.

"They were crying when their sons left, God is wearing black..."

They only played it the one time, and later that year Miles joined the Army. Could have been the couple months buying diapers on the wages of a fry cook and a sex shop clerk is what made his mind up. There was about a week there where Miles would let me borrow their car if I'd drop him off at the sex shop, just so it wouldn't be sitting, waiting for the repo man. Their phones were shut off most the time. I guess he saw a commercial one day and showed up at the recruitment office the next. This is back when America was balls deep in Iraq and a lot of niggas I knew couldn't piss clean were joining up no problem. Miles was one of those they tossed to the frontlines off the jump.

Their baby girl was a couple years old when he came home from Iraq with half his face blown off. He had this picture printed off a throwaway Kodak from right after the explosion. What happened was the Humvee he was riding gunner on had run over an IED. The Humvee flipped over and sent Miles flying across the desert and when he landed, he says he hopped up—half his face peeled off his skull, just dangling from his chin—and he says he upped his M4 ready to blast any haji in sight, but wasn't nobody around except his own squadmates and some goats.

So he starts blasting at the goats. Kills them all just to watch something die.

And we all believed the story because I told you, Miles is crazy. The picture he showed us was after he'd been convinced to lie down in the back of this truck, and he's lying there with his body full of glass and metal, blood haloing his head and half his face blown off, and in the picture there's this beam of light shining through a hole in the tarp, like the finger of god stretching out to touch his forehead.

When they shipped him home, it was back to the same ole, same ole. The Army gave him a Purple Heart and his scarred-up mug scored him almost a thousand bucks a month. He started selling weed and making beats. I'd come over and we'd smoke the weed he was supposed to be selling and he'd loop whatever beat he was obsessively putting together while we played *Call of Duty*.

He and Tonya were always in a limbo between fighting or fucking, or they were off fishing at the beach. One time I dropped in and they were gone but the door was unlocked, which wasn't unheard of. I decided to just kick it until they got back. Hit a leftover dab off some tinfoil on the table and booted up the PlayStation. I was still customizing my weapon setup when I heard the tinkling of xylophone keys from down the hall. Got up to check it out. Baby girl was wearing a princess shirt and a puffy diaper and she was going crazy on the keys now, there on her bedroom floor encircled by a cyclone drop of toys and stuffed animals. I unlocked the baby gate and she waddled over to me with her arms outstretched and I carried her to the couch. Tried hitting up both Tonya and Miles, but their phone bill hadn't been paid.

We watched *Blue's Clues* until baby girl got bored of that, and then I found some crayons in the mess on her floor but no coloring books, so I sat her on the kitchen countertop and showed her how you could color on the formica and it would just wipe off. She thought that was fun and she kept grinning and scrunching her nose up at me, this little cute-ass kid with a bird's nest of black hair, and soon the counters were all covered in blue and purple squiggly lines and then she started crying.

I didn't know how to feed babies at the time so I searched for a pan and scrambled some eggs that were in the fridge and she ate those okay. I didn't know the rules about diapers or nothing so I left that alone until Miles and Tonya finally showed up smelling like beer and salt water, both of them carrying a cooler at each end. Miles was cheesing real big and said, "We caught a shark."

He opened up the cooler and there was a bright blue bull shark laying on a bed of ice. Its gills fanned open-shut and its eyes were wide and there was blood all in the ice water. Baby girl reached out over the shark for her momma to carry her. The only bruise on Tonya's face was smudged highlighter yellow, meaning it was old, meaning they'd been working through shit.

Miles dipped off to the kitchen and opened the fridge and hollered out, "Nigga."

I shut the lid on the shark and poked my head in to see what he wanted, and he was tilting a milk carton sideways to show the last little bit swishing around, and this nigga had the nerve to come at me talmbout, "You for real drink all the milk?"

The time I got to fight his ass, we were tailgating at a Texans game. Thing about tailgating is people get drunk, and when Miles gets drunk, it can go one of two ways: he loves everybody so much he could cry, or he's ready to throw hands. This was one of those times he was ready to throw hands. Thing you gotta know about Miles is after he became the scar-faced slayer of Iraqi goats, the Army was kind of his whole shit. I've got this Arabic script tatted down my forearm—*Haqq: la illaha il Allah*—that I'd put zero thought into. I was dating this Sufie Muslim chick at the time and thought the symbols looked cool and it was fun to say. But that night at the tailgate, my tattoo was a declaration of war against Miles. The veteran with the Purple Heart, the hero who'd left half his ugly mug on the other side of the world fighting for his country. I wasn't finna get bitched out, though, so when he started screaming the Arabic chants of the hajis who killed his frontline brothers, talmbout *"You know what that means, nigga? Huh?"* with his spit flying in my face, I was like *fuck it, let's go.*

Tonya ended up driving me home that night. I don't remember it, but I remember how my face felt the next day. And I still ain't gone to the dentist to get a bridge in my mouth. Keep telling myself I'm holding out to do it big, get a gold grill or some shit.

We didn't fuck with each other again after that. I heard through the grapevine a while later that Tonya wasn't fucking with him no more, either.

Thing about Miles is war didn't change him. He was built to be a frontline nigga shooting five-five-sixes at goats with half his face looking like Tetsuo: The Iron Man.

Last time I saw Miles, he was fishing. It was an even number weekend so he didn't have his daughter with him. Me and my girl had brought our baby boy down there to build sandcastles and let him feel the sand under his feet. He's six months old, so we stand him up with his little fists wrapped around our index fingers. We'd all parked there in the sand, just this side of where the tide was coming in, and when I looked up and recognized the truck, and the scar-faced fisherman waist deep in the ocean, my silent prayer was we wouldn't get our car stuck and have to ask him to pull us out. But nothing happened. Miles eventually threw his rod in the truck next to the empty shark-sized cooler and my girl and I rinsed baby boy's feet off in the tide and we drove off in separate directions without saying a word.

My girl was riding shotgun with control of the aux cord, and I told her to look up that joint "Soldier Side," and I heard it as if Miles was singing it, like I always will, and it took me a while to get back to my body.

THE ADVENTURES OF NAKED MAN

This one time, my older brother chained his girlfriend to the toilet and beat her half an inch from death 'cause some other dude's name kept popping up on her phone. She'd told him it was nothing. She'd told him don't worry bout it. Thing about my brother, though, is he worries a lot.

And this is old news, you feel me. I ain't snitching. Everybody knows. Kinfolk got locked up for beating on his girl and a couple months later, she had their baby, a boy. My nephew. He's four now and his daddy's locked up in Clemens again just like the first eighteen months of his life but it ain't for beating on his momma this time.

So, there's that, I guess.

You know those cones they got on playgrounds that you can stick your head inside of and hear your brother whispering "pussy fart" and "faggot" through another cone across the sandbox? You know what I'm talking bout, they're like two-way megaphones, connected by metal tubes that run underground, giving a tinny and muffled echo to the slurs you and your brother hiss back and forth between each other.

I think about those two-way cones when visiting my brother in prison. We sit across from each other on either side of a permanently fogged window and we talk through these phones that make our voices sound like robots.

"My boy needs a role model," my brother tells me.

I want to say, "yeah, me too," or, "where am I supposed to find one of those?"

I don't want kinfolk to worry bout it, though, so I tell him, "I got you."

Now, you gotta understand where we're coming from.

Anchor, Texas is a coastal town, half beach/half chemical plant/all sticky heat and tweakers with face tattoos that match the stickers peeling off their tailgates. Picture shotgun houses with chain-link fences, johnboats parked in scalped lawns, retired cop cars bought at auction rolling around on swangas blasting Sauce Walka. There's two railroad crossings, one on the South side just before the bridge and one on the East side running parallel to the ocean. You'll find yourself stuck at either of them no matter what time you try to cross, 'cause trains only run when you got somewhere to go, like when you reach the end of the playable map in a video game.

Out of bounds, kinfolk.

Why I'm telling you all this, bout where we're from, is part one: ain't no role models around here. We got coaches, preachers, hell—some of us even got daddies. There's something in the water, though—some amoeba or virus from all the sewage in the ocean, or maybe it's something in the air, whatever's inside those black clouds that steady pump out of the plant's vent towers—makes people do crazy shit. You'll catch coaches looking some type of way at the little girls running snake laps. You'll find preacher man stumbling out of the ice house off 35, or hiding his face leaving a room at the Motel 6. And if your daddy ain't made it past the tracks, he's somewhere between working shutdowns at the plant and cutting thizz with caffeine in a beachfront trap house. Or he's locked up in Clemens.

What exactly is a role model anyway?

But then, part two: every small town's got its own local legend, you know, to compensate. There was even a hot minute, back when me and my brother was kids, Anchor had its own superhero.

Naked Man.

Like every hero's genesis, the name stuck from all the headlines.

Naked Man Stabs Himself in Neck and Jumps Out of Apartment Window

This is how we found out Naked Man couldn't fly, but he _was_ invincible. Too, he was always wearing a different skin when he'd pop up on the news, so either he was a shape-shifter or Naked Man was more an idea than a person—a symbol that any aspiring hero could embody.

Naked Man Caught Running Down 288 Covered in Blood

This is how we found out he had super speed and could jump like Spider-Man. Me and kinfolk sat glued in front of the TV during the live chase, watching Naked Man leap over cars and eat rubber bullets and tasers like the shit was nothing. Cops from out of town had to get called in to help stretch the road block. Took clouds of tear gas and a baker's dozen shotgunned bean bags to finally drop him.

Naked Man Arrested with Freezer Full of Cat Heads, Tests Positive for PCP

We all knew the heads were planted. Naked Man was no ghoul. But the same crooked media tryna take down a hero spilled the sauce on what gave him his powers, and now we could all be like Naked Man.

Personally, I got the inspiration whooped out of me that Halloween, which I told Momma she was wrong for, before getting whooped again for talking back. But it really wasn't fair. Some of my friends were going as their favorite superheroes too.

I truly don't know.

What even is a role model?

I take my brother's boy down to the jetties and we throw pieces of bread out on the water for the birds. He's too little to cast a line out just yet, much too little to reel in anything worth keeping. And I don't want to teach the boy catch-and-release, always felt that was cruel.

I play the good music for him in the truck. ICP, Three 6 Mafia, Korn. I tell him his momma ain't gotta know everything bout when he's with his uncle, but also, he should listen to her.

She don't like taking the boy to Clemens for visits. Hardly goes herself anymore. She don't like talking bout what happened, when she found out bout his alter ego.

The boy is learning his letters, though, so maybe he'll write his daddy one day. I encourage him to draw. He's starting to get into superheroes.

Halloween rolls around, and I ask to tag along to Spirit and show him the animatronic monsters, the rubber body parts, the costumes. He freaks out over a Spider-Man costume. Pretends to shoot webs from his wrists while hissing through the gap in his teeth.

I don't know what a role model looks like, but I think the boy will be just fine.

CAMBION

They rolled into town beneath a corpse grey sky, morning fog parting like stage curtains to present Boogie Woogie's Traveling Theatre. Starred-and-striped carriage drawn by two half-blind horses, one making up for the lack of the other. The driver of the carriage was Boogie Woogie himself. Or, had been, before he'd become what he was when we met his posse of insane clowns: a slumped stack of bones dressed in a baggy pastel suit.

Inside the carriage, Danny Cade massaged a fresh ulcer in his gums with a cocaine-dusted fingertip, while Tiny Tom and Daisy the Bitch slept off the bottles that rolled and clanked empty across the floor. Jack Morgan sat on the bench opposite Cade, balancing the sharp tip of his hatchet on his middle finger, then flicking it up into a spin and catching it by the handle. Grease-black smile painted over a tight-lipped frown; diamonds painted over bloodshot eyes.

Whole town was caught in that state of dream where the noise of the real world starts slipping in. Those of us who'd made our beds in the mud were still blinking flesh flies from our eyelids, while patrons of the saloon's upper rooms untangled limbs from one another to stretch, breaths rank with musk and thighs slicked in the juices of cheap pussy.

At the site of the clowns rolling past the grocer, the trapper, the whorehouse, we fisted our bleary eyes to focus and, one by one, fell into stupefied shuffle behind the carriage, whole town sauntering entranced as if tugged along by phantom ropes, lured by Boogie Woogie's posse past the bank, the jail, the stables, all the way out to the cemetery at the base of Chapel Hill.

It was there that the half-blind horses somehow knew to stop, even though the bone pale hands that held their reins remained still. Dead. We stopped there too, all of us. From the hilltop sanctuary, through a window hazed with morning dew and streaks of muck, Father Henley gazed down in the same curious hypnosis as the rest of us.

We could hear the clowns barking at each other. *"Whoop-whoop!"* one of them hollered, and another responded in kind. Then came the meow of rusted hinges and the iron drumroll of chain unspooling as one of the carriage walls dropped into a platform, held up four feet off the ground by a chain-and-pulley rig. The letters spelling out Boogie Woogie's moniker fell backwards in a muddy puddle, and there in the shade of this theatre box stood the four clowns, each of them possessing the drip and swagger of a shit luck drifter, devil red eyes betraying their painted-on smiles.

The midget was first to take the stage. In slurred baritone, Tiny Tom said, "Boogie Woogie's Traveling Theatre presents," and then he doubled over retching. Showered those of us closest to the stage in mud-colored bile that reeked of rotgut. We wiped our faces and spit out what we caught in our mouths and some of us who had only witnessed this started gagging and soon there was more sick than mud to go slipping around in.

Tiny Tom stuck out his chest and clenched the lapels of his coat. He carried on with the presentation as if nothing happened.

The play was called *Cambion*.

"What's that mean?" whispered the barber to a whore.

"I look fucking Mexican to you?" said the whore to the barber.

The butcher held a fat, scarred finger to his lips and shushed them and they shushed because the butcher was a giant who liked to cut once-living things to pieces.

On stage, Daisy the Bitch funneled fistfuls of salt into the shape of a pentagram and stood in the center of it and stepped out of her dress. Her body was death pale and fragile as a china doll—could count her ribs from where we stood—and when she kicked the dress out into the crowd, none of us ran hollering for it, waving it over our heads or sniffing it. We let it fall in the muck and watched as Daisy licked the middle and ring finger of one hand before shoving the fingers up her pussy, index and pinky fingers pointed out like horns. When she pulled her fingers back out, they were dripping blood. She used the blood to paint herself redder than the devil, dipping her fingers back in when she had to for more, then rubbing her hands slicked with crimson all over her stomach and thighs, her ass and tits, all the way down to her toes and up into her hair.

This is how the play began.

Jack Morgan, the hatchet man, stood at a corner of the stage and narrated with his head hung low, his teeth clenched.

This first act, he said, was called "Bastard." The story he told was of a woman who'd been having an affair with a demon while her husband was away at war. The woman had conjured the demon herself out of a deep and desperate loneliness. Daisy the Bitch, portraying the adulteress, whispered something in the tongue of chirping cicadas, then lay on her back just outside the pentagram and bucked at the air, eyes rolling back in her head, the cicada-speak of some wicked chant rattling off her tongue. A cyclone of flames spun up out of the pentagram before being blown out by a sudden gust of wind and in the dissipating cloud of black smoke on stage stood Danny Cade as the demon. A pair of ram horns were affixed to his head somehow, nest of yellow hair hiding whatever rigged crown he must have been wearing, and he was naked as the woman he immediately fell on top of.

Their hips rattled against each other like a pair of fighting bucks. Daisy yelped with each thrust and Cade threw his head back and howled.

"This affair carried on night after night for nearly a year," said the hatchet man, "until a letter found its way to the woman. War was over; her husband was coming home. The woman was struck ill with guilt and the life that'd been growing inside of her. She banished the demon before birthing its spawn alone in the bed she'd soon welcome her husband back into."

Daisy the Bitch lay on her back with her legs spread towards us, so we could see Tiny Tom's fingers spread her pussy open from the inside; watch him slip out like a snake shedding its skin... hands first, then black hat, then clown face, until eventually he crawled all the way out of her and she quit hollering.

"The woman never looked her child in the eyes," said Jack, "afraid to see herself reflected in them. Afraid of the devil. Before her husband returned, she swaddled the babe in the sheets she'd bloodied with birth gore and dropped him on the steps of the church and ran into the cemetery to watch from behind a gravestone, to be sure her devil child could cross the threshold of the house of the Lord."

Danny Cade played the role of the priest, stepping out from behind a tattered curtain to scoop Tiny Tom up off the stage floor and cradle him in his arms. Tiny Tom wailed until Cade's bouncing and shushing calmed him, and then he reached a hand up to stroke the clown priest's face and the clown priest beamed at the clown babe with a big yellow grin.

"The priest could see the boy had the devil in him," said the clown narrator, "but he saw the boy was still a child of God deep down, and so as the boy grew, the priest did everything in his power to feed the God part, and to drive the devil out of him."

Danny Cade kicked Tiny Tom across the stage, end to end. Tiny Tom rolled and cried out please and prayed for God to help him. Danny Cade said, "Don't you take the Lord's name in vain, crying out to Him with a devil's tongue." Then the clown playing the priest yanked down the pants of the clown playing the child and knelt behind him, unbuckling, and Tiny Tom went on crying and praying and choking on his own snot and tears.

A handful of us in the crowd dropped cold right there in the mud. Some puked. The barber chuckled, nervous perhaps. Don't know what the hell he could have found funny. The butcher curled his lip in disgust and walked back to his tent. As the play carried on, we caught him watching still, pretending to be more interested in sharpening his knives. Up in a grimy church window, we could see Father Henley looking on as well, no expression on his face.

"Every day," said Jack, "in the house of the Lord where he resided, the priest did his best to beat the devil out of that boy. Screamed the devil out of him. Raped the devil out of him. And every day—" without raising his head, Jack nodded toward the hills overlooking town, "—the boy would dream of running up in them woods and setting fire to everything."

Time became slippery. The clowns moved as silhouetted specters through the white hot spotlight of the sun, which now hung directly over center stage. The shadow of the church steeple stretched through the middle of the crowd and we all shoved for shade inside the inverted cross.

The play entered Act Two: "The Farm."

This act featured Danny Cade as both the Farmer and the Debt Collector. Tiny Tom continued his role as the Devil Child, and Daisy the Bitch played the Farmer's Wife.

Jack Morgan, knuckles white around the handle of the hatchet at his side, told the story while the other clowns acted it out.

"One day, in his ninth winter, the boy worked up the courage. Disappeared into the hills. He ate ice patties and slept buried under blankets of snow, but the hunger and the cold still got to him. Bloodied his mouth and withered him down until he was a walking corpse, the devil inside him the only thing keeping him upright. He made his way to a farm and collapsed inside a pig trough, closest thing to a cradle he'd ever

known. The pigs made a fuss about him the next day,
which raised the farmer's suspicion, and the farmer
and his wife took the devil boy in, cooked for him and
gave him a bed. The house was cold and the bed was
no softer than sleeping on the ground, but here the
boy could shut his eyes without fear of being eaten,
and he liked that these folks didn't care to touch him.
The farmer and his wife hardly ever looked at the
boy, save for stealing glances out the corners of their
eyes when he gnashed and gnawed on fried salt pork
and pan hoss. The boy had only known honest evil by
then, had yet to learn that the kindness of strangers
ought to warrant suspicion. Never crossed his mind
why there might be three empty beds fit for children
in the farmer's house, and no sign of any children but
for him. The boy didn't think to wonder where the
pigs come from neither, but how could he have known
this wasn't a pig farm? The pig farm was down in the
valley, an entire night on horseback away. The boy
knew this because when the pig farmer dropped in for
a visit, he apologized for his poor manners of riding
up in the middle of the night, 'It's just that, the ride up
here is long and unpredictable,' is what he said to the
farmer and his wife after waking them with his heavy
pounding on the door. The boy had watched them all
converse at the dinner table through the keyhole of the
room he stayed in. 'How are they?' the farmer's wife
had asked, and their midnight guest had responded,
'Oh, they're fine boys. They know their place and they

work hard and don't give me no lip.' The man had been smiling, but that faded now as he turned to the farmer, said, 'They must take after their mother.' He said this like it could have been taken in jest or as an insult, but he didn't care how the farmer took it. This man owned the farmer, the boy would soon come to find out. You see, the farmer, he liked to play poker. Or he used to, when folks would let him sit and throw down on a game, back when he still had anything to throw down. The wife felt that what the farmer truly loved was not poker, but punishment. The farmer loved to lose, and the only reason the boy could figure he hadn't lost her too, is she didn't have the devil in her, telling her to run out in them woods, die in the snow, and keep on moving anyway. 'Well,' the man who owned the farmer said, 'let's see it.' And the farmer went and fetched the child they'd found in the pig trough. 'Hm,' the man grunted, sizing up the boy. 'You can take twenty off the debt.' Then he turned and walked out into the snow and called for the boy to follow. The farmer rushed out instead, wondering, begging that they trade instead. 'That feral little shit ain't worth the backbone of your youngest,' said the man, already mounting his horse. 'Throw him up here in the saddle with me. Take twenty off your debt.' The boy was standing outside with them now, bare feet in the snow, every inch of him colored pink or blue with cold. His eyes, though, had gone full black, so the man and the farmer and the farmer's wife could see the devil inside him, could maybe rationalize the sudden fate that would be falling upon all three of them."

Addressing the crowd without looking up at us, Jack Morgan said, "The farmers' fate don't warrant depiction. You folks cling to whatever fantasy my vagueness might inspire, and by this tale's climax, we'll see just how imaginative you are."

Dusk fell. Sky the color of raw meat. Jack Morgan raised his head finally and, from where we stood, it looked as if his pupils had swallowed the whites of his eyes. "This final act," said the clown, "is called 'The Devil Goes to Church.'" And then he stepped off the stage, the filth of the earth squishing beneath his boots. "The devil child ran until he was hardly a child anymore," he said. "All he'd ever known bout the world is it will fuck you, try to kill you, and if you ain't ugly right back, it'll succeed at both. So the child grew ugly. He stole, killed, and he set fire to anything that'd catch just to watch the world burn, one piece at a time. One night, sleeping on a bed of ash in the scorched ruins of a lumberjack's cabin, the devil was awakened by the clomping hoofs and drunken howls of a carriage cutting its way through the woods. He took the hatchet from the dead lumberjack's back and walked out and stood in the road to meet the carriage. A boisterous fag with the face of a clown yanked the reins and hollered for the blind horses to stop. He looked down at the devil wielding the hatchet and said, 'Christ almighty, ain't you bout the ugliest sumbitch

I've ever seen.' Then he barked out a *'whoop-whoop!'* and voices inside the colorful box he drove barked back in kind. Then three more clowns climbed down from the carriage and stumbled drunkenly around to see the devil for themselves. The fag driver said his name was Boogie Woogie, and this posse of clowns was his traveling theatre crew. They were headed everywhere, nowhere in particular. Said the devil was welcome to tag along, so long as he painted his face and helped to come up with dramas for the posse to perform. The devil thought on it a bit. 'You travel all over, huh?' is the first thing he asked, and then, 'Could we incorporate some fire in these dramas?'"

This whole time Jack Morgan had been narrating act three, Danny Cade, Tiny Tom, and Daisy the Bitch had been slithering through the crowd. Eyes in the dirt, hands crossed behind their backs, respectful of the performance carrying on while anxiously awaiting its conclusion. Tiny Tom whispered around looking to bum a smoke, and the third one of us he asked—not one of the whores, but the cripple who mopped the saloon you could've mistaken for one of our whores—was ready to oblige with both the cigarette and a match. Tiny Tom tipped his hat in thanks and waved at Jack with the cigarette and stomped up Chapel Hill while savoring a deep drag.

Jack Morgan—the hatchet man, the devil—turned to follow the midget with the cigarette up to the church, and the rest of us kept close behind.

Jack went on narrating as we walked: "The devil rode town to town with the clown posse, from Bodie to Tombstone, all the way out to Santa Fe and back around, putting on magical shows anywhere they sniffed industry... mines and railroads, the gaming boat docks... places folks with cash ought be persuaded into giving spirits by a bit of entertainment."

Here, Jack paused, stood on the steps of the church and turned to us. He read the question written on all of our faces—'so why in the fuck stop here, in crumbling, cursed Buttfuck, Arizona?'—a question we needn't verbalize before Father Henley timidly opened the door with his eyes cast down, his jaw locked, a shiver in his step as if the spirit had taken hold of him. He asked the clown named Jack Morgan, "Does the prodigal son return with a heart of forgiveness, or condemnation?"

The devil answered the priest with a hatchet to the face. A wet crunch and a stripe of blood and Father Henley's eyes went crossed, mouth agape, face froze in a silent scream. He staggered backwards down the aisle, clawing at the tops of pews for support, and Jack followed in a patient and amused two-step glide.

Tiny Tom remained posted outside on the steps, taking a deep drag on the cigarette and then blowing out into the crowd. Taking over as narrator, the midget clown with the voice of a cancer-stricken mongrel said, "The sheriff of Buttfuck was then presented with a dilemma: engage with the devil, and die in the name of duty, or join the crowd in astonished adoration of the performance of a lifetime."

We all turned to the sheriff, who stood in the center of our hillside congregation. For what felt something like a minute or two, he just stood there. Tiny Tom passed the smoke to Daisy the Bitch, who took a drag and passed to Danny Cade. We swatted at flies and rubbed our saddle sores and spat in the dirt. Sheriff never spoke a word. He just tore the badge from his lapel and dropped it and walked away and that was the last time we had a sheriff in Buttfuck.

We turned to the clowns, faces expressing an eager plea for permission, and Danny Cade nodded. We stampeded up the steps, all of us all at once tryna squeeze through the church door. Daisy the Bitch said, "Enjoy the show."

Father Henley was on his knees before the devil, Jesus looking down on them both from the cross. The man of God choked a stuttering 'p-p-p' and the devil reached both hands inside the trembling priest's mouth, gripped the top and bottom rows of his teeth, and yanked in both directions. A few of us flinched at the snap. Father Henley's jaw hung loose, swinging on its hinges. The devil kicked the priest in the ribs until he fell sideways, and then he kicked at him some more, forcing him to roll from one end of the altar to the other, and then he tugged his pants down and kicked him again so that his broken and bleeding face was planted in the carpet and his exposed ass was up in the air. We stood on our toes to peer over each other, tryna see if the priest was even alive still, if the hatchet buried in his head hadn't finally split his skull and touched his brain. We couldn't be sure from where we stood, and didn't dare move any closer.

Jack Morgan grabbed the gold statuette of our Lord and Savior off the prayer shrine and rammed the son of God head first up the ass of Father Henley.

That gave us our answer. Father Henley howled.

The devil worked the Jesus statue in and out, twisting as he did, a kind of ecstasy in his blacked out eyes. He kept at it until the man of God quieted, until all the blood ran out and his eyes rolled back and he was dead. Then Jack Morgan pulled the tiny gold Christ out with a loud wet plop like when you flick the inside of your cheek.

The clown turned to face us. Blood dripped from Jesus's head to his feet. The clown clutched the golden Savior to his chest and took a bow.

THE SNOWY GRAVES OF CAMP BRAGG

San Juan Harbor, Puerto Rico, September 1918.

Hugo Irizarry spit a bronze string of blood into the ocean and threw up his fists. His vision split—too many knuckles flying at his face again. He blocked a fist that wasn't really there and watched the world spin backwards.

The head of a loose nail stuck him in a lower vertebrae and he lay breathless for a few seconds, glaring at a blurry flock of seagulls—their caws like mocking laughter.

Cash slid across palms in the crowd.

Jadier Figueroa took his cut with a bowed head and a solemn expression, then helped his beaten friend to his feet, still holding the money in one hand.

"I can't believe you bet against me."

"We can't both be broke." Figueroa waved half of the bills in Hugo's bruised face.

Irizarry snatched and pocketed the cash.

Figueroa kept a few paces behind Irizarry, eyes narrowed at the creaking planks of the dock, his mind weighing heavy on something. When Irizarry noticed he'd been talking to his shadow, he stopped and turned to Figueroa, said, "*Oye*. You didn't get your brain knocked around your skull. *¿Por qué te mueves tan lento?*"

Figueroa caught up to him and the two resumed walking. Irizarry bent to pick up a canvas bag out of a johnboat tied to the dock. Backhanded Figueroa on the arm.

"Spill it."

"I've been thinking."

"Don't hurt yourself."

"*Oye*, shut up. I found this way we could make some money, see, there's been ships carrying people to the States for work."

"What kind of work?"

"Well, it's kind of like, the army—"

Irizarry spat. "Fuck that. I won't fight for the country *que robó la granja de mi familia.*"

"No, no, no," Figueroa waved a hand back and forth, shook his head. "No fighting. With the war going on, they need laborers back home. We would be in a factory or something."

Irizarry glared. The rage boiling in his blood deepened the color in his eyes.

Figueroa draped an arm over his friend's shoulder, said, "Believe me, I feel the same way. But..." He tilted his head and shrugged. "They pay thirty-five cents an hour. Shelter you, feed you—"

"Are they paying you to recruit?"

"I'm just tired of getting beat down."

"The kid caught me on a bad day. I might have undercooked the fish last night."

"I wasn't talking about the kid, hermano."

They ascended the steps to the street and looked in opposite directions.

"*Disfruta tu noche, mi amigo*," Figueroa said, holding his hand out. Irizarry shook it. "Think about it."

Irizarry turned his back and waved him off. He grumbled under his breath and his stomach growled back.

Hugo Irizarry lived with his mother and daughter in a house with four metal walls and a metal roof and a cedar plank door that let the heat in. It was big for a tin can, but small for a home.

Esmeralda Irizarry sat on her heels in the front yard, using a stick to draw fish in the dirt.

Hugo smiled at the little girl as he walked up the hill to her. "Hey, mija."

Esmeralda squinted up at the shape of her father blocking out half the sun. She saw the bruises and cuts across his chin and cheekbones. "What's the other guy look like?"

Irizarry chuckled and knelt beside the girl and she jumped in his arms and he closed his eyes as her little hand traced the rough terrain of his face.

His mother came out of the house and stood with her arms crossed. The lines in her face told stories of lifelong struggle that was juxtaposed by the gentle warmth in her eyes. Irizarry stood and hugged his mother. She studied his face, but made no comment. Instead, she nodded to the canvas sack over his shoulder and asked what he'd brought for dinner. He handed the sack to his mamá. Scratched his arm. Looked at the ground, then off at the ocean in the distance.

Mamá turned from her son to hide her disappointment. She knew how hard he tried, and it wasn't always dwarf mullet, but most times, it was. She filleted and pulled the bones out of the skimpy fish then cut them into chunks and threw the chunks in a pan that sat over burning wood on a metal tabletop and then she squeezed lemon over the fish. It was a terrible way to eat the mullet but they didn't know of a good way to eat it and it was better than picking bones out of their teeth between each bite.

When the plates were served, Mamá took an old wooden chair, Esmeralda sat cross-legged on the floor, and Irizarry leaned against a wall and they ate it up quick.

Hugo's mother told Esmeralda to tell her father thank you and she said, "*Gracias por el pez, papá*," and Hugo smiled and winked at her.

Later—when the sun dipped lower behind the hills so that its orange hue still shone but its heat was less direct—Hugo and his mother sat on the porch, absently watching Esmeralda play with some of the other kids from the village.

Irizarry pulled a small flask from his pocket, unscrewed the cap. He took a swig and passed it to his mother. She grabbed it without looking at him and gulped a couple ounces down and held onto the flask.

"I know you have to make money, mijo, but could you bring home one of the good fish every once in a while?"

"That was the day's catch."

"*¿El dia entero? No vendiste nada?*"

Irizarry shook his head. He watched Esmeralda stick-fighting against two boys. Her stick was bigger. She was winning.

"Mamá..."

"*¿Que, mijo?*"

"Jadier found a job, said he could get me one, too."

The flask stopped at her lips. She looked from the corner of her eye at Hugo. "Where? How long?"

Hugo shrugged. "*No lo sé, pero escribiré cartas.*"

Mamá lowered the flask, stared at the ground. She tongued her teeth, thoughtful. "Is it a good job?"

"It's legal."

"That's not what I asked."

Hugo turned to his mother and they locked eyes and he said, "It's better than nothing."

She nodded and they killed the rum together and thought no more of struggle. The stars came out and

Hugo called Esmeralda inside and tucked her in bed
with a story of a man who left his family to chase a big
fish that—when eaten—would grant them wishes.

There were as many men on the cargo vessel as could
fit and they were all told the same thing: that they'd
be working in Southern states—in a climate that felt
familiar to them—but days passed, sleeping on wood
crates, and Irizarry and Figueroa were among those
standing in the open air when the mist off the waves
that slapped the ship's sides turned icy, bit into their
cheeks. The air was changing. The men shuffled closer
to each other without speaking of it.

They stepped off the boat onto a snow-covered ground
and were told to get into a truck that was just a flat,
metal bed with no cover and they shivered as the wind
bit into their faces.

Puerto Rico didn't have winter. Sometimes, the air
would be a little less humid, so you could sweat
without choking on it, but there was no snow.

North Carolina was going to be a different kind of
hell for the men who came up from the island, and the
cold was only the beginning.

Irizarry buried his chapped lips and cheeks in his
shirt collar. Kept thinking about the thirty-five cents

an hour. Imagined his daughter in a classroom wearing a clean dress and new shoes, his mother searing chunks of tarpon over the fire.

Figueroa's hoarse voice pulled Irizarry from his daydreams. "*Pronto, ya no tendremos frío.*"

Irizarry's stomach growled. "*Espero que haya mucha comida preparada para nosotros.*"

The first thing any of the laborers did upon arriving at Camp Bragg was stand shivering in a line outside the mess hall that backed out to the road they were brought in on and curved along the fence line. Irizarry leaned against the cedar wall of a barrack, hands cupped to his mouth, clouds slipping between his fingers. There were slits between the plank siding of the barracks wide enough to stick your fingers through. No insulation. Mattresses thin as the crackers the laborers got with their soup.

"Soon," Irizarry said, "we will no longer be cold. That's what you said." He slugged Figueroa and Figueroa massaged the stinging in his shoulder and toed the snow. He scowled at the ugly white powder that blanketed everything.

Before the military base, there were several acres of woods—dense with trees—and now timber and brush covered the campgrounds and it was the job of most every man who was brought up from the island to clear the debris. Work went like this: if you were given an ax, you used it to chop the fallen trees into logs small enough to be dragged or carried away, and if you didn't have an ax, you dragged or carried the timber to the burn pile. Orange embers jumped from each chunk of wood tossed in the fire and floated away with the snow. Each trip to the burn pile meant a moment of warmth, so you made a big circle around the flaming brush—like a planet orbiting the sun—making the moment last as long as it could, which was never enough. Ax heads struck fallen timber in syncopated thuds. The men you thought to be sergeants turned out to be contractors of James Stewart and Company—hired to cuss and holler at you between sips from canteens tucked in their fleece sweaters. Of this particular task, they were committed. They'd do all the barking while treating you like a dog. You'd drown them out by focusing on the crackles of the growing fire, the whistles in the wind. You sucked cold air into your lungs in raspy wheezes. You thought of home—of mornings waking drenched in sticky sweat—and you missed it. You thought of your daughter drawing pictures in the dirt with sticks. You chopped, chopped, chopped at a tree on the ground, gazed around at all the others lying in the snow. You would stare up at a sky that looked like the underside of a frozen lake and you would try to catch your breath while wondering where the sun had gone. A foreman barked. A hand fell heavy on your shoulder. You followed your ax to the ground.

The base hospital was a long metal building shaped like a split log. Beds lined the walls, most of them occupied by men still in their work clothes. Irizarry woke in a coughing fit, startling Figueroa, who sat in the bed next to his friend's, his leg in a splint.

Figueroa slapped Irizarry on the back a few times, said, "Let it out, hermano, let it out."

Wheezing exasperated, lungs rattling against his ribcage. "I feel dead."

"I thought you were. You've been in here three days. Doctor said it's pneumonia. You're not alone, either."

Irizarry looked slowly around the room. In every bed was someone hacking up their insides or tossing sweat-drenched in a nightmare-filled sleep. He rolled and touched his feet to the ground and his head swam. "Chinga—"

"Here." Figueroa grabbed two white pills off the rusted metal table between their beds. Handed one to Irizarry, swallowed the other dry.

Irizarry looked from the pill in his palm to his friend. "No water?"

Figueroa nodded to a medic stitching up a man's hand. The medic sewed the needle and thread in cross patterns through the man's palm, pulling the split skin together over the bleeding gash. The man groaned and dug his heels into the bed. When the medic finished, he cut the thread with scissors and dropped the needle in a cup of water. Rust-colored clouds swirled around the needle. Then he took a cotton ball and dabbed it in the copper water and swabbed the man's wound.

Figueroa said, "*No quieres beber el agua.*"

Irizarry's lip curled. His throat felt like sandpaper. He raised his palm to his mouth and paused. "You have pneumonia, too?"

Figueroa shook his head. Pointed at his leg. "Broke it dragging brush to the burn pile. Stepped wrong in a hole. *Estúpido pendejo.*" Figueroa forced a laugh. His sunken eyes were red, slick with tears he fought back. "We have to get out of here, Hugo. Rent a cheap room in town or something."

Irizarry stood and stumbled in a circle, braced himself on the edge of the bed. "We have to work to get the money to get out of here," he said. He gently patted his friend's wrapped leg. "Hurry up and get better, amigo."

Figueroa nodded, his mouth open but not sure what words to say.

Irizarry staggered past a handful of medics who paid him no attention. He told one nearest the door that he was checking out and the medic nodded and waved without looking at him. Irizarry said, "*Folla a tu madre,*" and the medic nodded and waved again, then rolled his eyes and sauntered over to a patient thrashing in his bed.

Irizarry stepped outside. The brightness of the sun bouncing off the snow pierced his eyes. Everything went blurry. He took two shuffling steps and fell face down in the snow.

Irizarry tossed from fever dreams for several days and when he came to his senses, the room was filled with darkness. He bolted upright, whispered Figueroa's name, then shouted it. No answer, no sign of his friend. He ran outside, forgetting his boots.

"Jadier! JADIER!"

The brush fire was taller than the barracks now. Irizarry ran through the silhouetted groups of men swinging axes and dragging brush, grabbing each of them by the shoulders, studying their faces. One of the laborers grabbed him by the arm, said, "Who are you looking for, hermano?"

"Jadier," he said. "Jadier Figueroa."

The man's face twisted in a way that made Irizarry's chest sting. He pointed to a field covered in crosses made of branches. Mounds of overturned snow and dirt covered the fresh graves. Irizarry ran through the crosses, row by row, until he found the one with his friend's name written in charcoal and he fell to his knees and wept until the men who barked orders came and forced him to his feet.

Hugo Irizarry swung his ax into a fallen tree. With every swing, his chest felt like it was cracking open and any moment now, he expected his heart would burst out and he'd swing his ax at it so it wouldn't hurt anymore. The foreman assigned to bark at them for the day had refilled his canteen twice in a span of an hour and every worker he got close to could smell the whiskey emanating from his pores. He was barking especially loud today. Irizarry saw the man's face contort and spit fly from his mouth with each slur he spat, but all he heard was the gentle ebb and flow of the waves beneath his boat. In his mind, he was back home. He was out on the water with Esmeralda and Mamá and they each had a line cast, waiting for a bite. He kissed his daughter's head and squeezed his mother around the shoulders. Esmeralda jerked forward, caught herself. Her stick was bouncing up and down and she stood in the boat, wrangling a big one, saying "Help! Papá, help!" Irizarry held his daughter around the waist and said, "You can do it, mija," and just as the fish was about to break the surface, Irizarry was thrown to his back in the snow. The drunk stood over him and threw a fist against his temple. "You don't get paid to daydream! Wake up, you dirty bastard!" Irizarry took one more blow to the face before the man backed up and Irizarry stood. The drunk shoved an ax at Irizarry and he took it, wiped tears from his cheeks. "Back to work," the drunk said, and Irizarry caught the faces of the men around him—saw the rage reflected in their eyes. He swung his ax into the foreman's face and it made a wet cracking noise and split open in a diagonal line just below his left eye to his chin. Blood spilled over the ax head and fell like crimson rain drops over the snow. The other workers dropped their axes and rushed the man with a battle cry that their friends beneath the ground could hear and they shoved the man into the brush fire. Irizarry staggered back and sat on the tree they'd been chopping. He snapped off a limb and used it to draw a fish in the snow.

THE FUTURE

I leave the old man clutching his throat, trying not to bleed all over the mahogany floors. I'm doing enough of that for both of us, my sprint to the front door marked by a long red stripe, the blood spilling from where I chewed off my front right paw. For a stupid moment, I wonder if it'll grow back, if I'm quick enough for that. Halfway down the driveway, though, I'm just hoping I don't bleed out before the change.

The iron gate at the bottom of the hill winding up to the old man's mansion is there to keep people out, not wolves in. It's easy enough to slip through.

I force myself to make it to the cover of trees before shedding the beast.

It's hard to say what happens first, it's all so—well, not fast, not at all, but so—all at the same time.

Every muscle, every bone.

The worst part, though?

Imagine your face getting smashed to pieces, those pieces being jigsaw-puzzled into a shape close enough to resemble what you last saw when you looked in a mirror. Imagine a mask made of raw meat and baby flesh being pulled snug over the cracked sculpture of your new-but-familiar face. And whole time, you're thinking of how a newborn's skull cracks open so its head has some give on its way through the birth canal, how it forms back together on the other side, but not quite all the way yet—that soft spot taking maybe a couple years to find sanctuary under bone. And—remember cutting teeth? At least that was one or two at a time, right?

Yeah, everything about the head is usually the worst part, but this time, everything south of my right wrist is confused—the nerves lassoing the bone, the flesh stretching and shrinking, unsure of where to sew itself shut.

The dirt is soft and I want to sleep away the throbbing, the hunger, but I remember what I'm running from, that I've got miles to put behind me before shutting my eyes.

I stand on shaking legs, pinball between the redwoods for balance.

My feet are blistered and shredded by the time they touch asphalt. I realize I'm shivering, probably have been for hours, judging by how chapped my lips and shoulders are. I use my arm to shield my eyes from street lights. Where I'm at is a convenience store parking lot, which means security cameras, night owls, a clerk with a shotgun under the counter.

Wolf hunters who hype up silver bullets have never tried a .12 gauge at close range.

I'm already turning back towards the woods, thinking I'll stalk behind the tree line for a less populated area to emerge—what I should've done in the first place—but it's too late. I hear the screams, the rapid footsteps, the slamming of car doors. I turn, see the young couple's faces through the windshield. They wear the expressions of the faces in my nightmares, of all the people still chasing me out of town, no matter how far away I get. Pressed to the passenger window as the car peels out in reverse is a phone capturing everything—the dried blood around my mouth, the nub where my hand used to be, my dick—it'll all be on the internet by tomorrow if I don't do something about it, now. So I run out in front of the Prius and the driver slams on the brakes and the next thing pointing at me from a window—driver's side, this time—is a .38 snub nose, aimed at the constellation of bullet scars around my ribcage. The hand holding it is shaking.

The wolf inside me grins.

The kid's phone says my destination is on the right. Already hearing sirens, I park the Prius a couple blocks up, on the next street over. Double back on foot.

The kid's shoes didn't fit and I didn't feel like chewing my toes off, so I'm still on bare feet. Might as well still be naked, his hoodie stopping at my forearms and navel, his jeans too tight to zip up. I'd let him keep everything else, including his life and his girlfriend, so he should count himself lucky that of all the wolves in the world, he met the one that wouldn't eat him. At least not in a public, lit parking lot, and not in this state of exhaustion.

Looking up and down the block, I realize how far from home I am. Maybe an hour to the motel—and I don't know if the motel counts as home, yet, or if it will be much longer—but, still, this is what some folks call a nice neighborhood—rows of town homes and fenced trees planted in straight lines along the sidewalks, no vagrants barking in their sleep, no car alarms going off. Feels like another planet.

I whisper the house numbers to myself until I find the one I'm looking for. I crawl on all threes up the steps to the front door, because I'm too tired to stand or because I forget I'm not all wolf, all the time—either is true.

I use the doorknob to pull myself up. Slouch against the door. Knock with my forehead, like a sad pup in a kennel.

I can hear her inside, walking on her toes to the door, her breath like a knife unsheathed when she presses her face to the peephole. There's a series of clicking and sliding sounds and then she's standing in the doorway, the lack of color in her face a sharp contrast to her burgundy nightgown. Hand at her mouth, trembling.

I force something like a smirk, say, "You've seen me worse," and my knees buckle and I reach for the door jamb with the hand that isn't there anymore. She catches me at the waist, leads me inside, locks the doorknob and the deadbolt and the chain before leading me to the couch. She sits in a white cushioned chair that's shaped like a tear drop.

There's an oversized clock on the wall above where I lay. Floating shelves hold thick encyclopedias. A small shark swims around inside the coffee table, staying close to the glass walls.

Now I really do miss the motel.

"Your drive to the office must be a bitch," I say. "Thought I remembered the wrong address for a second."

She sits leaned forward, arms on her thighs. She's yet to blink. She looks at me like I'm something she's never seen before, like a ghost maybe, not like the injured werewolf she's used to seeing.

I say, "Doc," and after a few seconds of silence, "Vanessa."

The color rushes back into her face. She blinks, straightens her spine. Asks if I want a water.

I say, "Try again."

Vanessa gets up and walks to the kitchen without ever turning her back. She returns wielding two tumblers of whiskey, hands me one of them. She sits leaning forward again, swirling the rocks in her glass.

"What happened?"

I kill the whiskey in one gulp and place the glass on the aquarium table. The little shark inside is magnified as it swims beneath the tumbler. I search my memory for a minute, trying to figure out where to start.

"I was hunting. Caught a four-point, tasted as good as he looked. I was burying him, thinking of keeping the antlers, wondering if it'd be disrespectful to do something like that; trying to convince myself the buck would be honored, somehow. I don't know. Out of the dark, something bites me in the ribs. All my muscles tense up and I hit the dirt. Someone walks towards me, but I'm sideways, can only see their shins down. I remember thinking how clean her shoes were. She must not have been walking around in the woods for long."

"She?" Vanessa says.

"Yeah," I say, pointing to my nose. "I can tell."

Vanessa shifts in her seat, doesn't press it. She says, "Then what?" The ice melts in her whiskey. She hasn't taken a sip.

My eyes grow heavy and my vision splits everything in two. I put my face in my hand.

Vanessa sets her glass down and kneels next to my head. She pets my head and makes shushing noises.

She asks if I want painkillers, or a sedative.

I tell her yes, all of it. "And," I say, "I need some blood tests or something. I blacked out in the woods and woke up in some basement, garage, I don't know. Looked like an abandoned warehouse, but also like a cave. This old man—he did stuff to me. Had me hooked up to all kinds of drugs that kept me weak, kept me chained to the wall." I unzip the hoodie to show Vanessa the scars. She gasps, and the hand that was petting me now digs its nails in my scalp. I say, "I was there for so long, it felt like. I'd died and this was hell. The drugs did nothing after a while. I was awake the last time he cut me open. That woke the wolf up, too. And that part was so much worse than usual, especially the mouth—it's like I was trying to grow more teeth than my mouth could fit, little razor teeth. And I couldn't breathe. Thought I was going to suffocate, that was going to be the end. You know me, though. I've never tucked tail."

I reach for Vanessa's hand on top of my head. When I look up at her, it's like seeing her face through a kaleidoscope. I try not to vomit all over her white furniture or her shark tank coffee table. I try real hard not to. When I can't keep it down anymore, Vanessa runs upstairs.

My muscles melt, my bones turn to iron.

The shark swims behind a waterfall of puke.

Vanessa runs back downstairs, and from where I lay sideways, I can only see her from the shins down. She's wearing white cargo pants now, and white shoes that have the smell of bleach on them. I hear her grab her car keys, then her hands are under my armpits, dragging me off the couch and out the back door. She grunts and drops me several times trying to get me in the trunk, but eventually she succeeds. She either thinks I'm not conscious to any of this, or she has a lot of faith in whatever high-grade tranquilizer she spiked my drink with.

She keeps saying sorry.

She says something about me being an important part of the next leap in evolution.

She closes the trunk.

I wake up back at the mansion, back in the basement or garage or whatever part of the mansion that smells like death and medicine, but instead of shackles—the old man was smart enough not to gamble on me chewing off any other limbs—I'm inside a cage, one of those deep sea diver types, the door at the top of the cage chained and padlocked.

Below my ceiling-suspended cage, a shark swims around inside a topless tank just big enough for him to swim circles in. If he wanted to, he could probably get enough momentum to launch himself over one of the side walls of the tank, but I guess this shark isn't thinking of suicide, yet. He must be new.

The old man types at a computer somewhere below. Scattered all over the concrete floor are metal tables adorned with saws and scalpels, shark fins and organs. It smells like an underwater morgue.

I whisper down to the shark, "Hey, want to blow this joint?"

The shark just keeps swimming in circles.

Footfalls ascending metal stairs.

The old man appears in my peripheral. He's on a platform about six feet up and a few inches out from the shark's tank. The bandage around his neck is stained brown over his throat. I smile, happy with myself, only a little bummed I didn't rip his voice box out, as a trophy. Or a chew toy.

The old man dumps a bucket of chum into the shark's water. I wonder how high sharks can jump.

Wolves can jump pretty high, when we want to.

I glare at the old man like, *put me in that tank, let's see what happens.*

I say, "You should see a doctor about that bite. I know a really good one."

And this is where the old man slowly makes eye contact, smiles with one side of his mouth. He bends down and picks up a rod that reaches all the way through the bars of the cage, even with my back against the furthest side. The rod touches my chest and lightning shoots through my bones. I fall to my knees, go wolf to man to wolf over and over again, each time more painful than the last, until the world goes black.

I dream underwater. Swimming in circles inside a tank too small to do anything else. The old man stands on the other side of one of my glass walls, wearing a smile that would tear his face in half if it were any bigger. Vanessa stands next to him, gazing wide-eyed at me, shaking her head. She's smiling, too. Her voice muffled by the glass and water, she says, "Can he change?"

The old man thinks for a second, tilts his head side to side as if to say, *yeah, maybe.*

The old man walks away and comes back with a bucket, which he hands to Vanessa, who is eager to take it and run up the steps to the platform. Her shadow walks across the floor of my tank.

I don't know how high sharks can jump, but I know what a wolf can do, and when I crash into the cloudy red water with the top half of Vanessa's body in my mouth—the sound of her bubbling screams vibrating through my skull—I'm not counting how many teeth I have, but I'll always be more wolf than anything.

Gas Tank

The night she came home covered in blood, dragging the severed head of a parade float Santa across the garage floor, I stopped kidding myself.

Our relationship's origin story was the typical 'meet online, drive across the country to see each other, move in together within a week' tragedy. I'd conjured up fantasies since seeing her picture on Craigslist, and meeting her IRL didn't shake me out of that dreamer's delusion.

My phone quickly filled with selfies of the two of us doing the most menial shit—getting drive-thru ice cream, barbecuing on the front lawn, bumming at the beach.

Oh, yeah. I was *that* guy.

But, could you blame me?

I'd begun to look the way I lived, on pizza and booze. Ten years at the chemical plant had aged me twenty.

Crow's feet.

Sleep apnea.

But she—she had that classic kind of beauty. And, the way she moved when she let me inside of her—it was a rush of new life, like being hooked up to jumper cables. Each time made my legs shake, made me tighten my grip around her.

There were those nights, though, I'd wake up to headlights illuminating the curtains, rush to the window to see her creeping down the street. And then, when she was out of sight, I'd hear that roar, and my eyes would roll back and I could feel phantom vibrations up my spine.

I never questioned where she went. As long as she kept coming home, it didn't matter. I'd help her wash the blood off, kissing every inch of her body as it was washed clean, and my own suspicions and judgements would simultaneously be washed away.

So, no, I never called the cops.

They showed up on their own, though, that night she made an appearance on the live action news. Headline: *Christmas Parade Massacre.*

They asked to see my car and I said, "Um, yeah, sure thing, officers," and when the garage door rolled up, I fake-gasped, acted like I was so fucking shocked to see an empty garage. I guess they bought it. I filed a report about my car being stolen, said "thank you so, so much" and "please, bring my baby home."

I knew she'd be back.

Soon as I saw the head bouncing between the concrete and her undercarriage, with the Santa hat and face full of white scruff, I knew the cops would be back, too.

So I did the whole *throw your hands in the air and scream WHAT HAVE YOU DONE* routine; paced around the garage, ripping fistfuls of hair from my scalp, while she just idled there in silence. Broken teeth and brain matter on her windshield.

If this was going to be the end, it was going to be the absolute fucking end, so I grabbed the lighter fluid and she revved up, blinked a couple times to show approval. I covered us both, getting high off the fumes.

I popped her gas tank and said, "One last time, baby?" and she purred.

Yes. One last time.

JELLYFISH IN GEOMETRY

Fry stands in the space of what used to be a wall, judging from the mountain of bricks sloping four stories down to the street. He sips some kind of sludge that smells of fish and grass from a blue willow tea cup and he says to Slim, "Yo, check this out." He wipes the sludge that dribbles from the corner of his mouth with the back of his hand, points at the apocalypse orange sky, says, "You see the ripples?"

Slim sits Buddha-posed atop a dogpile of combusted bodies. He leans forward so that he's talking into the microphone hanging from the ceiling, its cord wrapped around exposed conduit. Gasping in feigned shock and clutching his chest, he says, "*Mortis circulos.*" An inside joke he doesn't care to explain, since the audience is dead and the microphone isn't even plugged in.

Fry laughs like it's the first time he's heard it. He remains in the space of the blown-out wall, sipping sludge from fine china while gazing out at the city, round shades reflecting flames that spiral and swell like flowers in bloom. "I tell you about my dream?" he says.

Again into the microphone, Slim says, "The one where you're gay? Yes. Many times."

"We were on a beach," Fry says, "just chilling on the worn cedar porch of this little shack, and we were watching the waves roll in and crash against the shore, but the weird part was every wave brought like a dozen jellyfish to spit out on the beach, so there were hundreds of jellyfish just fucking everywhere, right? The whole beach was covered in these gelatinous pulsating frisbees, like you couldn't walk if you wanted to without stepping on one, and you were going on and on talmbout the 'jellyfish in geometry,' and in the dream I was like, 'damn, bro, that's bars,' but when I woke up, I couldn't remember what you meant by it."

Slim scoops a Raiders cap off a blackened skull smiling up at him. He punches the top of the hat so it goes inside out, puffing a cloud of ash, and then he slips it onto his own dome, pulling down until it fits snug with the brim just above his brows, casting the top half of his face in shadow. "What *is* the geometry of a jellyfish?" he says, raising a fist to rest his chin on. "Pancakes and squiggly lines?"

"Nah, that's not it," Fry says, now pacing the loft cramped with charred corpses, his steps kicking up little cyclones of ash to swirl about the concrete floor. "You weren't talmbout the geometry of jellyfish, it was something bout jellyfish *in* geometry."

"Oh, bet," Slim says, "like bone-in chicken."

Out in the street, an old man shuffles past the smoldering wreckage of roasted commuters. Cars and buses all smashed to shit, contorted and accordioned around street lights/palm trees/other vehicles. Bird's eye view of city traffic looking like colorful crushed soda cans. The old man is peeling off layers of clothing as he drags his feet, leading with his head, soldiering on by sheer force of will. His insides are burning. You can tell by the diamonds of sweat glistening all over his body, or how he's coughing up smoke. He's down to his boxer shorts and he's heading in the direction of the ocean. With the wall blown out, Fry and Slim can hear the old man from up in the warehouse loft, muttering, "Goddamn, it's hot," before the now familiar pop and shockwave of human combustion that begins with the old man's face going all puffer fish, his torso and arms ballooning until he bursts into a ball of fire, cindered bones collapsing there in the street.

Ripples of the blast crawl up the warehouse, vibrating the remaining walls. Slim hums the bass riff of a Queen song. "Da-da-dum... dum... dum..."

Fry lurks near the banquet table. Places his empty tea cup between a pitcher of fentanyl lemonade and a candy dish full of cigarettes. "So what's your verdict," he says, "aliens or God?"

"You are so far away from the mic," Slim says. "I don't think it's picking you up at all."

Up against the furthest wall from the door is a piano, where one of the combusted sits slumped over the keys, wearing nothing but stained briefs and a gold chain. Blackened crispy body spotted with patches of bright pink flesh. Fry runs a finger across the high notes. Kicks a loose high heel across the room. "Maybe we should try going back," he says. "Assuming, you know, we haven't combusted yet."

"Fuck it," Slim says. "This party's dead." He leans in closer to the unplugged mic, so his lips are now touching the metal windscreen, and he says, "That's it for this episode of Sporescapes. Drop a line in the comments if you're still with us out there, and check out our merch at www—"

Fry steps out through the cavity in the wall and floats up into the orange sky until he shrinks out of sight.

Slim is less theatrical about returning to his body. On the throne of crispy corpses, he shuts his eyes and focuses on breathing. He imagines each breath drawing him closer to where he left himself slumped in a bean bag chair in a Koreatown apartment on the opposite coast. Somewhere in the dark behind his eyelids, he hears the melodic chirping of his phone going off. Fry calling to say he made it back okay. Slim takes another deep breath—inhale... four, three, two... exhale—and he opens his eyes.

FLESH AND BLOOD

Evelyn studies the sun glowing on her son's cheeks.
It's the two of them, three depending how you look at
it, on the pier behind their trailer home. The rod in
Timothy's hand bends forward. Bends at the waist like
a nimble pole dancer. That's how his mom would put
it, at least, but Timothy has no clue about that.

Or maybe he does.

Who knows how much he really knows.
Remembers.

But he's fighting with this pole—

"It's a big one, Mom!"

—and Evelyn, Mom, she's sitting on the bench her
husband built for times like this.

Speaking of Cade, yeah, he's there too.

Not in spirit, not if you ask Evelyn, but in flesh—in
a way.

Those glowing cheeks.

The way Timothy struggles with his pole, wrangling
this catfish that keeps jumping up out of the
water—hook in mouth—to mock the kid, this scene is

projected onto Evelyn's irises. Like a grindhouse flick, the footage vibrates, the film melts, cut scene.

Flesh footage, all of it.

Fingertips skating down Evelyn's back as she drifts to sleep, Cade's fingers sliding under her nightgown, circling her navel, flicking the ring that dangles there. This scene, it always goes one of two ways.

Evelyn grinning, hand heavy with sleep pushing Cade's fingers back to start position.

"Nuh uh," she says with her eyes closed, scooting closer against his crotch, rubbing her back against his hand. "Just rub it, baby."

Or.

She takes his hand, eyes still closed, grin spreading the way her legs do, guiding his hand south.

In both scenes, the ending is the same. Evelyn falls asleep smiling. Cade kisses her forehead, slips out from under the covers, and the shed light stays on all night.

Off screen, real life, Timothy is saying *help, Mom, he's too big, help me pull him in*, but this is background noise. Silence in the theater, children.

On her iris screens, the film melts. Changeover. And this is noise footage, speckled with grain, showing its age. It's the backseat of her mom's luxury SUV, the one she raced down Staggs for money. Cade's on top of her for the first time ever, hands shaking. Evelyn puts her tongue in his mouth, her hands down his basketball shorts.

A flash across the screen, blink and you miss it, shows a broken arm. Instead of bone, it's splintered wood jutting from beneath the skin.

Blink and it's gone, cut to the SUV rocking in a ditch, waving at the cars passing by.

Off screen, Timothy's line snaps, and there's that flashing image again.

Splintered wood/tattered skin/Christmas lights on the ground.

The catfish swims home.

"What the fuck, Mom?"

Timothy throws his pole down and stabs Evelyn with his eyes, that sharp stare, tearing into her iris screens as he walks past, exits theater left, retreats to the trailer. Slams the door.

Still sitting on the pier bench, the hazel projectors Evelyn's spinning reels on play deleted scenes. Outtakes and gag reels. Real funny stuff never before seen by an audience. Yeah, haha. A clip of Evelyn in bed, Cade crawling under the sheets. Evelyn's hand on his face, pushing away. Cade digging knives in her skull with his eyes, cutting deep as he walks to the door, narrow pupils dragging a sharp tipped blade across her face with each step.

Evelyn winces, never cries, not with tears, but her face says please, stop hating me, and her mouth says, "You don't have to go."

Spit flies from Cade's mouth when he turns on his heels in the doorway, says, "Well, I can't stay."

"You can lie next to me without fucking me," Evelyn says. "I don't feel good."

"You never feel good."

The shed light stays on all night. Cade pounding out a cacophony of hammer blows.

Pillow folded over her head, Evelyn doesn't sleep.

Hammer pounding, pounding.

Evelyn lies with her knees in her stomach. A black monster munches on her ovaries, takes a slice from her uterus. Dining in, as always. Leaving her womb empty as the second bedroom in her and Cade's first real home together.

A wood panel box with mint green freckles where the beige is peeling. A neighborhood where the buildings all tell the same story and cedar fences slouch further forward every time it rains. After that first month—the insomniac mechanic across the street, the Tejano music blasting from the backyard next door, the windows getting smashed in—it's all white noise.

But hey, ask Cade, it's better than their apartment. Better than waking up thirty minutes early in case a tire needs to be changed, because almost half the complex drives the sunburned Civic and pissed off exes never read license plates.

Ask Evelyn, too, she'll tell you. At least she's not hiding a cleaver in the laundry basket to take a trip to the laundromat. At least it's not years later, living with Timothy in a trailer by the river where he dives in to drown himself, instead just floats out in the middle and bakes in the sun until burning pine-scented sweat seeps through his pores.

Evelyn standing at the edge of the pier, shoulders slumped, chin to the sky. Shouting for Timothy to please come in before he rots.

As if he knows what she means by that. This is before the splintered arm. Long before guzzling termiticide to kill the hungry bugs in his bones. Worries for another day. He always swims back in, eventually. Always limps back to their trailer, the rusty hinges of his joints locked up again. Limping the way his father did every time he came back in from the shed, another part of his body bandaged.

But no questions from Evelyn. Never any questions.

When the bandages made their way over his fingertips, up to his neck, when Cade was calling in sick more and more and Evelyn was calling in favors from her mom to pay the bills more and more, there were still no questions. Not from Evelyn, or from Kandy Kayne, the name she used when sliding down a pole. The name on her work schedule, her pay stubs.

No. No questions.

And no more begging mom. Fuck that. Evelyn's a grown woman, damn it, she'll pay her own bills. Even if her husband is too much of a mummy to roll out of bed any more.

He still does, though. Every night, slipping out from under the covers, limping to the shed. Sounds of hammer blows replaced by buzzing saws.

Buzzing, grinding, shredding.

Timothy's door is closed. Like father, like son. A screaming banshee escapes his stereo, slides under the crack in his door, rattles the walls of the trailer. On Evelyn's bedside table, a heart shaped locket vibrates and falls to the floor. Pops open. A strip of paper flies out, handwritten cursive blurred as it spins to the floor, lands face up. Eisley. The ghost white peanut cradled in the locket, her name would have been Eisley.

Retina projections across iris screens, fade to black.

Evelyn wakes up on the pier. She winces at the pink morning light striking her eyes, holds her hand over her face until they adjust. That transition, like coming out of a dark theater in the middle of the day.

She walks in a daze to the trailer home, pulls the vibrating screen door open.

Black metal/Timothy face down in bed/drenched pillow.

Evelyn kills the music and stands over her sleeping boy. Strokes his hair. Closes her eyes. Touches his cheek, sticky and wet with tears. Amazing, the way he can produce those. Such craftsmanship, this boy, her husband's greatest creation.

Evelyn stops at her open bedroom door, her throat knotted, and she stares at the open locket on the floor.

Dragging feet/wet eyes wide/hard swallow.

Evelyn bends and puts the pieces back in the brass heart locket, holds it shut against her chest. She sheds a single tear and takes a deep breath.

The shed light stays on all night.

Ice windows/plant corpses/grass blades with white tips.

Timothy never asks about the bandages.

All winter, every night, the shed light stays on. Evelyn never asks how.

Chemistry textbooks/empty Sudafed boxes/plastic baggies of what looks like rock candy.

The time Timothy breaks his arm, first broken bone in his life, is the first time his mom says anything to him in months.

Timothy biting his lip. Evelyn staring with her head cocked sideways at the blood dripping from her son's chin.

"Incredible," she says, and with a mummy-wrapped hand touches her mouth, the only part of her still exposed aside from her eyes and ears.

Timothy cradling his shattered arm, helping himself up from the bottom of the porch steps. Half of the Christmas lights are still hung, the other half coiled over a collapsed ladder on the porch. Instead of bone, what juts from Timothy's skin is pine wood splinters. He and Evelyn are both in the shed that night, Timothy sitting on the work bench, Evelyn gluing and stitching his arm back together. Bandaged fingertips sew shoddy needlework. When it's done, Timothy has large *x*'s pinching his arm flesh shut.

And Evelyn's hand goes back to her mouth, her hazel eyes mesmerized by the dry blood on her son's chin. And Timothy, he rotates his arm in front of his face, his bottom jaw dangling from its hinges.

Pushed up in a corner of the shed are a couple of saw horses, a sheet draped over whatever project lies on top of them. Evelyn's secret. The shape of this thing under the sheet, the curves—it's almost the shape of a girl.

"Mom...what have you been working on out here?"

Evelyn's lips: a quivering smile, then a sour pucker. "Let's go inside," she says, "I'll make dinner tonight."

Evening primroses crawl up out of the green grass.

The first morning of Spring, a note scribbled in chicken scratch sits in the center of the kitchen table. Timothy rubs his eyes and peeks in Evelyn's room. The bed is empty. Sheets lie tangled on the floor, spread out to Timothy's feet at the threshold.

"Mom?"

Timothy twists the blinds open, sees the shed light is still on. Mom must have pulled another all-nighter.

He pops his termiticide capsules with one long chug from a water bottle and turns on cartoons before picking up the note on the table. When he does pick it up, his lungs inflate and hold a single breath as he reads.

The first line scribbled across the top of the page: *We always wanted children. I couldn't give that to your father, not until I figured out how he gave me you.*

Such craftsmanship, the way his eyes produce tears as Timothy reads how before his father was a surgeon, he was a carpenter. The father he never met.

The mother he'll never see again.

There's a knock on the front door. Timothy chokes back the last of his tears, wipes his cheeks with his sleeve, rips the note and drops the shreds—lets them fall like glitter in a strip club, or sawdust on a shed floor—and he swings the door open.

A girl stands on the porch in front of him. Hazel eyes. A line of *x*'s stitched under her lips. Resting against her chest on a chain necklace is a heart shaped locket.

"Evelyn?"

"Hello, Cade," the girl says, her lips quivering into a smile.

The way their brass hinge joints bend perfectly to wrap wooden arms around each other. Such craftsmanship.

Hurricane Season

I couldn't tell if it was the ghost or the wind doing all the howling until another cat smacked against the window. This time it was a soggy black cat with bulging green eyes. Stayed pinned against the glass for several seconds before the wind peeled its body away and sucked it back up into the grey sky. It was the third fly-by cat since the storm had touched land. Marcel was rolling us a blunt on a Ouija board, chopping the shit with a planchette. He licked the leaf and pinched the blunt closed, said, "This shit might get nasty." I started thinking he was probably right, but I was cool with it.

If you take 288 south of Houston and hop off onto 35 before you hit the coast, cross the tracks twice and dip off the highway after the playground with the epithets keyed into the walls of the slides, but before the corner store with the broken pumps, the first trailer on the left on a road that dips a few extra feet below sea level is where we lived. It was right outside of city limits, meaning we were close enough to town to walk to the Valero for 'rillos and milk, but we could also shoot guns off the back porch and the neighbors couldn't say shit. It was the perfect set-up. I miss it all the time.

We had a plywood stash in the shed from the last hurricane.

Pieces cut to fit over the windows. We went around the trailer using a stack of buckets as a step to screw the plywood to the window frames. Marcel mostly held the bag of screws and shook his head at the weather radar on his phone.

"Nasty as fuck," he said, "what'd I tell you."

A plastic kiddie pool tumbled down the street beneath a sky full of black clouds.

We could have upped the bike into the trailer, easy. 250cc, only three hundred pounds or so to split between the two of us. But our generation was raised on *Jackass*, and lining up one-by-ten shelves taken out of the closets to make a ramp up the porch steps seemed a more interesting way to keep my bike safe from the wrath of god that was raging in from the gulf. Marcel recorded the whole thing on his phone, too. Me rolling slowly up to the base of the steps and backing up again, then repeat, getting comfortable with it. My dumb ass smiling and sticking my tongue out at the camera, signaling this is it, this is go time. Riding up the makeshift ramp like it's nothing, like I'm a pro, baby, except for that moment of hesitation that came both too late and too soon near the top step, and the camera moved from the blur of the bike tilting and sliding backwards to follow my body going over the side rail, Marcel behind the camera going *shit shit shit shit*, running over to catch the money shot of me looking up from my back, breathlessly insisting, "I'm good, I'm good."

Marcel cleaned his guns at the dinner table. I sat at the opposite end with a bowl of oatmeal. He had an arsenal: pump-action .12 gauge, carbine rifle with the laser sight, Draco. Plus a few different pistols and revolvers, one of them a pearlescent rainbow-colored .357. The walls had a low vibration to them. I asked if this still made sense, what we were doing.

Marcel worked a pipe brush through the barrel of a .40 aimed at his eye. He said, "You scared of a little wind and rain?"

"We could sell on the road," I said.

"Hotels and fuel are up to storm rates, cous, the overhead would be loco." He sort of sang the word *loco*. Then he pulled his phone out, said, "Best we stay off the road anyway, at this point." He pulled up a video someone had posted of the evacuation route to

Dallas. Endless rows of brake lights shrinking into the misty grey horizon up I-45. Everyone going zero miles an hour. "Now who do you think is more vulnerable, huh?" He grinned. "Fuck outta here."

Marcel put his phone away and wiped the .40 down with a sock.

I finished the oatmeal. Grabbed a pipe brush and a disassembled revolver and got to work.

"What's all this for, anyway?"

"What do you mean?"

I waved the revolver around, motioning to the guts of all the weapons strewn across the table.

"Some people meditate," Marcel said, "I do this."

I shrugged. After a minute or so, it made perfect sense.

Marcel's insurance plan was in colorful baggies pregnant with weed and X. Baby bottles full of purple stuff chilling in the fridge. Orange pill bottles with handwritten labels. "When this shit clears up and niggas come home," he said, "I'll be the only one not waiting on the re-up." He grinned. "I'ma be the Scarface of B-County."

I said, "You know how that movie ends, right?"

"Shit's like, three hours long," he said, "fuck I look like?"

We filled a black trash bag with our dirty clothes and tossed the bag in the back of Marcel's 300 and drove to the laundromat. Something that should have been done before the storm was already creeping up on us, but what do you do. Must have been, we were too busy making deals with the plug and getting laid off from our jobs to think about having clean clothes, so there we were, driving down 35 with the wipers on full blast making it even harder to see through the windshield. Rain coming down in sheets that billowed in the wind. Sign posts bending backwards. Foam cups and crumpled chip bags flying through the air.

Marcel kept a death grip on the wheel, trying to keep us from hydroplaning, then trying to just land straight when it happened a couple times anyway.

The laundromat was a 24-hour self-serve type of place. Whoever owned it didn't have to stick around for it to remain open, which of course it was. And we weren't the only patrons dripping puddles onto the black and white checker tile. There was the chick with the cotton candy-colored mullet sitting crisscross on top of a rattling dryer, reading a manga, and there was the tank top bro with biceps bigger than my head folding baby clothes, air-drumming to whatever was playing in his earbuds.

Marcel held the door of one of the front-loads open and I untied the bag and tossed the clothes in by the handful. I wondered how long it would take before the shirts I wore to work didn't smell like fire anymore, now that the steel fab shop was closed for good, since the boss had said another hurricane was too much to bounce back from and pulled the doors down. It's an almost spiritual experience, watching a man with an assault rifle sewn onto his hat weep in the company of a dozen people he'll forever owe a final paycheck.

Marcel played a game on his phone. Another phone fell out of a pair of jeans I tossed in the machine and clattered on the floor. Marcel said, "Oh, I been looking for this," and he bent to pick the phone up off the tile. Slid it into his back pocket. Went back to his game.

The job thing didn't worry me.

I'd probably just slip back into the two-phone life myself.

We sat with our backs to the floor-to-ceiling windows getting hammered by rain. I watched the machines rattle. Marcel hadn't looked up from his game.

He said, "I tell you I got a picture of the ghost?"

I said, "For real?" I blinked at him, then at the phone in his hands.

He said, "Yeah, hold on a second."

He dragged his thumb across the screen. A long snake made of glowing dots bounced between blue and purple squares in zig zag patterns until all the squares shattered and the snake absorbed itself into a single glowing dot and a pop-up flashed the words 'high score.' An ad began playing and Marcel closed the game, pulled up his photos. Scrolled past rows of tits and memes. Zoomed in on a selfie he'd taken in the bathroom mirror at home.

Sure enough, there it was. A distorted, translucent face leering over Marcel's shoulder. If I didn't know better, I'd have blamed it on the camera flash distorting some smudge on the mirror, but I'd lived there long enough to notice the climate shift when the lights went out, the rummaging noises in the dark.

He said, "Tell me that shit don't give you chills."

I said, "You think it might be her?"

"Nah, doesn't smell like her. You remember that smell."

"Old lady perfume and Black & Milds."

"That's it. I'd definitely know if it was her." Marcel tucked the phone in his pocket and rested his head back against the window. Shadows of rain drops streaming down his face. "We gotta burn some sage or some shit."

I watched the clothes spin through the window of the rattling washing machine, trying not to see faces in the suds.

Back at the crib, Marcel played this video game in which he was an outlaw in the Wild West days. One of those open-world, do-whatever-you-want games. Marcel's bearded avatar rode his horse out to a lake and cast a line and we spent a good minute passing a blunt while Marcel waited for the controller in his lap to vibrate, letting him know he had hooked a fish.

I said, "You ever consider Bostrom's simulation theory?"

He grabbed his crotch and said, "You ever consider these nuts?"

The outlaw swatted a mosquito on his neck. Tugged his pole.

"We could be just like that guy," I said. "Artificial versions of our own ancestors."

The controller vibrated. Marcel pulled down on one joystick and spun the other and the outlaw started reeling in whatever was flexing his pole. Must have been a big one. Marcel leaned forward, eyes glued. Thumbs flicking the joysticks. The line snapped and Marcel fell back into the couch, said, "Damn." Then he pressed some buttons and the outlaw tossed a stick of dynamite in the lake and the water rippled with a muffled boom and the outlaw collected the dead fish that rose to the surface and then mounted his horse and rode off.

Marcel said, "The existence of you is the only truth you know."

I sat with that while Marcel lassoed a police officer and dragged him behind his horse. He went on, blunt bouncing between his teeth, talking 'bout, "Look, I don't care if we crawled out the ocean a billion years ago or we just some ones and zeros on the demiurge's desktop," he pinched the blunt and held it in my face, "this shit still hit right."

I snatched the blunt from him and took a hit. Coughed up a lung. The outlaw rode to a swampy marsh outside the city and hogtied the officer in the mud. Before long, an alligator came out of the water and ate the writhing policeman alive.

A million more feral cats slapped the barricaded windows. The barrage of thuds against the trailer became the chorus to the hurricane's song. Could have been tree limbs, I guess. I mean, yeah, probably. It's a distinct sound, though, the way a cat screams. I dunno, could have been the wind.

Sideways rain misted through the mesh screen. Everything outside the radius of the red porch light was edge-of-oblivion black. I counted the nail heads sticking up out of rotting floor planks while Marcel swiped through Instagram stories.

"This nigga, bro," he said, flipping the phone to show me. It was a rap video, done up all professional with visual effects and shit that made the rapper's necklaces look like they had real diamonds in them. I knew the dude. High school days. Marcel said, "You know your boy got robbed last month by some niggas that weren't even strapped."

There were several girls in the video. Knew at least a couple of them from high school, too. They all danced around with guns and stacks of cash. Dude rapped about street shit, made a lot of Houston references—swangas, syrup, Screw. Marcel said, "I don't get why he reps Houston so hard, like we don't live an hour outside the city."

"Doesn't he sell?" I said. "You can't sell and rep where you're from. That's like inviting the feds to your door."

"Feds don't give a fuck about this small time nigga." Marcel yelled at his phone, "We went to school together, bro! You cried when the principal called your momma! You not hard!"

I laughed. Bobbed my head to the music. "Not gonna lie, though," I said, "dude can spit."

"Spit a bunch of bullshit," Marcel said, now swiping through selfies of different women, pressing the heart button on almost all of them. He muttered, "Goofy ass."

There was a chittering noise coming from under the porch. Some creature sniffing out the kibble littered across the floor planks. Overturned metal bowl in the corner. Before the incoming storm blew all the feral felines out of the neighborhood, we liked to keep a few strays around to take care of the snakes. The paw reaching up through a gap in the floor didn't belong to a cat, though. Marcel dipped inside, came back with the .40.

I said, "You serious?"

He said, "What?"

The paw slid back into the darkness between the planks. Chittering continued. Marcel sat in his chair with the heater in his lap. I scooted my chair back a bit to be less parallel with the direction he might start shooting in, which would probably be the small hole in the screen, where the paw was now reaching through, stretching, widening the hole. A shoulder pushed its way through and then another paw and then a pair of glowing eyes was staring right at us. Marcel bit his lip. Brought the heater up slowly. The coon made it most of the way onto the porch before Marcel shot him in the head.

The coon dropped to his belly. Eyes closed.

Ears ringing. I asked Marcel if that was really necessary.

He shouted *huh?* 'cause his ears were ringing, too. So I shouted back.

When it was just the sound of the wind again, he answered.

"Those shits carry rabies, cous."

"Still an animal, though, I mean, come on."

"Nah. Dogs are animals. Coons are a nuisance. Like a rat. Like a giant rat with knives for fingers. They're like the Freddy Krueger of pests."

I wasn't sure I felt the same way, but I laughed.

And then the coon pushed himself up onto all fours. Half an ear missing, stripe of raw meat on the side of his head. Marcel had only grazed him. I mean, besides the ear.

The coon snarled and hissed, looking extra devilish in the red hue of the porch light. He stood on his hind legs, tall as a toddler. Marcel put a few more shots in his chest and the coon held himself and moaned, but remained standing there, dripping. Marcel blinked in disbelief. There was maybe a couple feet between us and the coon. Three .40 caliber rounds should have been overkill, but the thing was determined not to die that night.

I felt sick. Was about to dip inside for the shotgun, show the poor critter some mercy, but he gave one last hiss and dove back through the hole he'd climbed in through, left us with the smoke in the air and the blood on the ground.

Marcel said, "Cous." Jaw in his lap.

I said, "Motherfucker ate those bullets."

"Something ain't right in these woods, cous, I'm telling you." Marcel pulled another blunt from a jacket pocket. Lit it with shaking hands. Leaned back and blew smoke. "Something ain't right at all."

The wind howled. I closed my eyes, said a prayer for the coon, swallowed vomit.

Later that night, the sky fell apart. Downpour like buckets of nails being dumped from the clouds—*ting, t-t-ting, t-t-t-t-t-t-ting.* Colored pixels danced around the television and the lights flickered. The walls shook and dropped everything to the floor—the Basquiat paintings we'd printed off the internet, the pawn shop katana hanging over the sofa, a photo of Marcel smiling down at his grandmother, hugging the short woman around the neck, the flames of birthday cake candles lining the bottom of the frame. Hardest part about being stuck in a haunted trailer during a hurricane is you can't tell what's happening because of the storm, what's just the ghost doing ghost shit. We got in the tub together, just in case, our knees to our chests so both of us could fit. Marcel kicked my shin and said, "You want to light some candles?" and I said, "No, I don't want to light any candles," and he laughed and called me a faggot. The night would soon find us stretched out like sleeping crash test dummies with our faces pressed against the porcelain, legs tangled together, dirty socks in each other's faces. The walls still trembling as we slept like high little babies.

In someone's backyard stable, a horse bucked in the mud. Rain poured in through a tear in the tin roof, soaking the mound of hay left behind for the abandoned beast. The horse reared up and knocked the gate open with his front hooves and took off into the stormy night, sprinting full force against the wind and the rain, dodging flying Coke cans and ghost-driven tricycles. The kind of thing you see in those old cowboy paintings.

The subfloor creaked under phantom footfalls and the shadow people moved around on the periphery and the weed grinder kept shifting a couple inches to the left of where you last set it down. Maybe our ghost was feeling neglected, or maybe it was amped up off the storm's energy. We just let it go, because what the fuck else can you do? At some point, you learn to live with the things that haunt you.

It was crazy to imagine that in other parts of Texas, the sun was shining, and the streets weren't underwater.

The wind died down and the rain mellowed and a hot, sticky mist rose from the ground. Eye of the storm. We stepped out back for some air while we had the chance. Marcel sparked a blunt, offered me a hit, but I passed. Bored of the shit, I guess.

I stood at the edge of the porch and looked up 360-degree photos. Zoomed in on one of the Milky

Way. Waved my phone around while spinning in circles, exploring the galaxy in my hand.

I asked Marcel if he had any shrooms.

"Nah," he said, "too much liability. I can't tell the difference between the magic ones and the ones that kill you."

I said, "But you sell pills."

"Yup." Smoke cloud around his head growing larger. "Niggas don't give a fuck what's in pills, though. And there's no guess work in which ones kill you, 'cause at some point, they all do."

I looked up more places I'd never see in person. Explored the inside of an Egyptian pyramid. Floated over the edge of the Devil's Pool in Zimbabwe. Whole time aiming my phone at the ceiling or the floor or spinning around in circles.

Marcel said, "You look like a crazy person."

I said, "Wish I looked like a crazy person on shrooms."

"You seen that virtual reality porn," he said, "where it's like, you're looking through the eyes of the dude getting his dick rode on?"

"That's not a real thing."

"Real as fuck. On god, bro, look it up."

I made a mental note to do that later, alone in my room.

Marcel got to coughing, pounding his chest. He jumped to his feet and smacked my shoulder. Shaky finger pointing in the distance as he struggled to catch his breath.

I started to ask if he was good, but then I saw what he saw, just this side of the tree line. The coon was out there cupping his paws in standing water, washing out the triangle of bullet holes in his chest, the jagged crescent moon of what used to be his ear.

Marcel and I stared in awestruck silence at the coon that would not die.

The devil in critter form, the spawn of an ancient curse, the zombie coon.

The legend we'd tell forever, even though no one would believe it.

Cockroaches scattered across the floor and up the yellowing floral wallpaper. We chased after them, wielding shot glasses as traps. When each of us had caught a roach, we dragged our glasses side by side to where the living room carpet met the kitchen linoleum. That was the starting line. After *ready-set-go*, we lifted the glasses, and here's the thing about roaches: they don't give a fuck about racing, they just run, directionless, so we had to crawl behind them, keep smacking them onto the imaginary track. The race ended with numbers on a dumbbell stamped into my knee and Marcel sliding his hand into a work boot to hammer the roaches to death with, their nuclear war-proof bodies spiraling a foot off the carpet each time he slammed the boot down close, but not close enough. For whatever reason, neither of us felt like talking the rest of the night. We passed a blunt in silence on the back porch while I nursed my knee with a frozen burrito.

The next morning, Marcel sat alone at the dinner table and stared at an empty beer can. He had his hands on the table, palms down on either side of the can. I toasted a Pop Tart and spread peanut butter on it and took a bite. I said, "The fuck are you doing?" Tongue stuck to the roof of my mouth.

Without breaking focus, Marcel said, "Practicing."

"Practicing what?"

"Moving shit with my mind."

I left it alone. The vibe of another person can be exhausting to be around after so long.

I climbed over the back of the couch and knocked empty 'rillo packets off the cushions. Dug around for the remote. I turned on the TV and the room filled with hecklings of a disgruntled studio audience. Even louder, though, was the rapid aluminum clatter on the table. I poked my head up over the couch to see Marcel's right eye twitching, neck showing veins. Couldn't see what the can was doing. I turned the volume down a little. *Maury* was on. Some dude getting slapped and booed for the truth coming out about him fucking his wife's mom.

I took another bite of the Pop Tart.

The TV people had blurry mouths and spoke in bleeps.

I thought about this one dude we went to school with who had caught time for chaining his girlfriend to a toilet and beating her half to death. He'd been off his bipolar meds—some shit to do with insurance—and she couldn't eat solids for like a month. But she'd visit him all the time while he was locked up, and then the day he got out—not long before the hurricane hit—he moved back in with her. I wondered if they evacuated with family or stayed behind like us.

I thought about the widows and the loners, the folks who had no one to beat up on when they became overwhelmed with their own insecurities.

The people on TV cried and threw chairs. They said bleep you and bleep her and bleep your momma. Then they ran backstage and cried some more and hugged each other.

The can rattled on the table again.

The world outside was drowning and there we were, stuck inside watching daytime smut, practicing telekinesis with beer cans.

Later, I stepped out on the back porch to be alone, but the ghost had beat me to it. The night was so dark you could touch it and the wind was a soft, steady whistle. The air grew cold and the red porch light buzzed and blinked dim to bright, dim to bright. Thermometer nailed to one of the four-by-fours supporting the tin awning read just below a hundred. I touched my lips, could see my breath slip through my fingers. I heard from somewhere that ghosts are souls who refuse to move on, either tethered to this life by an unfulfilled purpose or in defiance of whatever comes next. I wished I could talk to our ghost, see what else we had in common. Maybe sometime soon, I'd brush the seeds and stems and 'rillo guts off of the Ouija board, give it an honest attempt. As it was, though, we just stood there in silence, staring back at the pair of glowing yellow eyes watching us from the woods.

It rained so much that the river broke the levee, so what we had then was the murky water from the Brazos pouring into the streets and blending with the rain water that had already pooled up to at least shin height in most places and just kept rising, rising. Marcel was out on the porch, being all emo about his car. I watched from behind the screen door as the water swallowed the tires and then crept up the porch steps until what Marcel was standing on was a floating platform. My heart broke for him, really, but all I could think about was the bike at the foot of my bed, how we weren't even thinking shit would get this far when we pushed it inside.

Boss Man lived in the woods near the train tracks. He always introduced himself by a different name—Barney, Freddy, Rambo—so folks just called him Boss Man, 'cause of the way he dressed, I guess. Plaid tweed jacket, duct-taped loafers, royal blue tie splotched with stains.

Boss Man.

He spent each night in a tent and bathed in the sinks of public restrooms. Spent most days in the vacant lot behind the library, getting drunk off donated beers, drawing with colored pencils, fidgeting with a blood-crusted box cutter. "For skinning rabbits," he'd say if he caught you looking. Jagged scar across his throat.

Boss Man.

Eyes milky and cracked at the edges. Broken teeth in his smile. Wrinkles on wrinkles on wrinkles.

Maybe he'd heard about the hurricane early enough and hopped a Union Pacific boxcar, rode it someplace far from the coast, someplace with mountains he could draw in pink and purple hues to reflect the sunset.

Maybe, yeah.

Boss Man.

Here's a question: If a vagrant drowns in the woods and no one is around to hear him, did he even scream?

If only we'd had a boat, or at least a semi-truck, we could have been one of maybe half a dozen groups by now to hit a lick on the corner store. The storm doors would have already been pried open for us to wade inside and snatch whatever was left above hip level. It was senseless to daydream about the cash box or the scratch-offs, or even the booze, probably, but—that glass tower with all the pipes and shit locked up inside it? There was this knife I liked to look at every time we went in there, had a handle shaped like bat wings and a hook at the end of its long blade. No idea what I'd use it for, just thought it looked cool as shit.

But we didn't have a boat.

Or a semi-truck.

So, yeah.

There are things that have been but never will be again, and there are things that never were to begin with.

We were watching *Adventure Time* when the power went out. With the plywood covering the windows, the inside of the trailer was a cave. That kind of darkness where your eyes are in a perpetual state of adjusting, shapes bending and floating around the pitch black room, the kind of shit you see when you shake your head with your eyes closed. The climate shift was instant. Muggy as a swamp in that bitch. Sleep would mean sweat-soaked sheets and fever dreams.

And without any electronic distractions, without the comfort of a light switch, it'd be harder to pretend that the phantom hands pressing down on your chest in the middle of the night, or the distorted silhouette standing in the corner—somehow darker than the inky blackness of the room—that those things weren't actually there. Just a trick of the light. Haha, what light? But fuck it. The ghost lived here, too. What did it for me—what stirred up the regret, the thought that maybe we'd have been better off road-tripping to San Antonio, or out to west Texas somewhere (they buy dope in the desert)—it was an icon on my phone's screen before shutting it off to save the battery, the one blinking *no signal.*

The horse lost his footing several times, stepping off of underwater curbs and dipping into potholes. Neck craned skyward, hair matted wet, the horse tread onward in search of higher ground. He came to a four-way stop where the water was almost touching the signs. A stream ran horizontally at the intersection. The horse gnashed his teeth and neighed at the rushing water as if to say *fuck you.* The sun was shining and the rain was coming down hard enough to sting. The horse rested his head on the branch of a willow tree in what used to be someone's front yard and he fell asleep standing up.

We sat in the middle of the floor in the blacked-out room, facing each other with flashlights under our chins so that the shadows distorted our faces all ghoulish, passing another blunt, trying to exhale the smoke in different ways over the bulbs of our flashlights—waterfall, dragon nostrils, rings—severe boredom type shit.

Marcel said, "You ever hear of the Process Church of the Final Judgement?"

I shook my head no and took a drag.

Marcel said the Process Church of the Final Judgement was this cult in the late sixties. He said a bunch of the members were camping in an abandoned salt factory in the small Yucatán village of Xtul when Hurricane Inez came through and fucked them up for three days straight and it was during this time that the cult formed its basic theology, which was pretty much that four gods lived inside of every person—Jehovah, Lucifer, Satan, and Christ—and that the unification of all four gods would manifest as perfect psychological balance. Pretty dope shit, except their best ideas were watered-down Jungian philosophy misinterpreted through the lens of ex-Scientology dorks who thought sex and drugs were bad and, oh yeah, who thought the perfect symbol to represent the four inner gods would be a swastika.

I coughed up smoke and passed the blunt. "Fucking hippies."

Marcel took a long drag and held it in his chest. Shrugged. "You tryna start a cult?"

We sat there for a minute without talking and every now and then, the floor would vibrate with the trumpeting of a massive wind blowing by.

God in the form of a hurricane.

Marcel said, "You want to burn some shit?"

I said, "Sure."

I followed him in the dark to his closet, where he had me hold the flashlight so he could grab a box from the top shelf. He grunted under the weight of it, said, "Let's go," and I followed him to the bathroom, where he dumped the box full of books into the tub. Books with Latin titles, mostly, some leather bound with no defining inscriptions, all of the pages yellowed. Grimoires. Magic books.

"Today's her birthday," Marcel said, taking a small torch from his pocket and touching the hissing blue flame to a corner of one of the books, tossing it back on the pile.

I said, "Renée?"

"All this haunting shit is her fault, you know." Torching another book, dropping it on the pile. "She played too much."

"This might make it worse, low key."

Marcel shrugged. "Makes me feel better." The amber light of the flames lit up the lower half of his face. He was grinning. "I tell you she sent a letter?"

"What'd it say?"

"'Miss you, love you' type shit. Apologizing for the way shit went down after Grams died. Guess she finally realized where she was at. The pen is fucking with her head."

"You going to write her back?"

"Nah, she'll be out in a few months. I did drop more money in the commissary, though."

There was a nice size fire going in the tub now. Black smoke drawing soot halos on the ceiling.

I said, "Probably better than a 'love you too.'"

Marcel said, "Hell yeah."

I had a moment of enlightenment—a moment of *fuck it, I hope it all gets washed away; I hope nothing goes back to the way it was; grant us the freedom of a clean slate, O great Hurricane; baptize us in your raging waters and renew our minds*—but that moment didn't last too long.

Marcel shone his flashlight at the wall and we made shadow puppets with our hands. Marcel made a wolf howling at the moon and I made a duck and he made a bird flapping its wings and I made a llama and he made a Samurai kneeling down and unsheathing a small sword to commit seppuku.

I stared at his hands, said, "How the fuck you do that?"

He wiggled his fingers, said, "Double-jointed."

The horse's flesh was blackened river rot, bubbling and tearing away from patches of raw meat. It was like that from his belly down. He found shelter beneath a strip club marquee, hooves splashing in low standing water reflecting neon pink lights. A mangled storm door floated around the parking lot. The club entrance was propped open by the ATM someone had given up on, thick chains coiled around the base of the machine. The horse made his way inside the club. On every wall, a mirror. In every mirror, a horse that should be dead. All at once, the herd of rotting horses reared up and neighed, hooves splashing back down in glitter water.

I worked the hand-crank can opener while Marcel lit a burner on the stove with a match. Flames shot out of the burner holes and Marcel went "ouch" and licked his fingertips. The storm was death-metal-coming-through-blown-out-speakers loud. We warmed up the ravioli and ate it out of the pot.

The trailer swayed as if on sea legs. Somewhere in the dark, Marcel was softly singing Kevin Gates. *"All my diamonds shine 'cause they really diamonds..."* Imagine a pecan tree uprooted and dragged through the street by the same wind knocking over lamp posts. A scalped-to-the-dirt yard littered with gutted cars—engine block hanging from a swing set, spinning on a rusty chain. *"They ask me if I'm high, I say, really really..."* Imagine waterfront houses bending at the stilts and crashing into each other like dominoes. 'Come and Take It' flag flying off its trailer hitch pole to be washed away down a flooded street. The cherry of a blunt glowing in a pitch black room. *"I'm really out my mind, I say, really really."*

Pacing in a room black as ink, thinking, *Is this still happening? Like, what the fuck?*

There was a sound like god's bones breaking and then a tree came crashing through the roof. Rocked the trailer as it split it down the middle. Splinters and little white drywall rocks and pink clouds of fiberglass everywhere. Daylight fractured through the branches of the tree that lay across the living room floor and there we were, glued to the couch in shock, staring through a curtain of heavy rain that fell from where there used to be a ceiling. We were stuck like that for however long it took until our feet felt wet inside of our shoes, then it clicked that this was real and we had to do something, had to get to higher ground. Marcel said, "Grab whatever you can't live without," the hardest part of which was climbing through the tangled branches to get to my bedroom at the other end of the trailer. The year before "cool if I crash on your couch?" turned into "here's my half for bills," I'd been hitching around the country, searching for I couldn't say what, but not finding it anyway. That said, I got used to living with light baggage. For our rooftop migration, the only use I had for a backpack was clearing the canned goods and protein bars out of the pantry. I had a lighter and brass knuckles in my pockets and I couldn't think of anything else worth saving. Marcel, though, he seemed to grab everything. Duffel over each shoulder—one full of guns, one full of drugs—and he carried a backpack stuffed with I don't know what, probably sentimental shit, or maybe just whatever fit in the bag. We made our way around like we were kids pretending the floor was lava, walking across countertops and couch cushions. We loaded a small Styrofoam cooler with the codeine baby bottles from the fridge. The water flooding the trailer was maybe knee deep, now. DVDs and picture frames and 'rillo packets floating around. We floor-is-lava'd our way to the tree and climbed up to the roof, where we shared the cover of a trash bag held above our heads.

The whole world was islands of rooftops surrounded by muddy water.

Marcel fell apart in stages. First, he rolled up a blunt. Sat crisscross with his back turned to the tree jutting up out of our home. The rain now a light drizzle, he looked up to the clouds and stuck his tongue out. I kept the trash bag draped over my head and dealt with my own denial. Marcel mumbled something. Maybe he was singing. Then he started laughing to himself until the laughter turned to tears. And I don't know if he ever even sparked up that blunt, but if he did, he never passed it.

Stage two of his falling apart probably started with him pissing through the hole in the roof, a steady stream running down the tree into our living room, just adding more to the flood. Mumble-rapping under his breath again. Pacing. I lay on my back with my eyes closed, trying to focus on the rain drops hitting my face, oblivious to what Marcel was doing next until the first gun blast gave a jolt to every nerve in my body. I turned my head to see Marcel shooting the limbs off the tree with the carbine. Each shot sucking all other noise out of the air. Bursts of splinters like fireworks. Marcel maimed the tree until the clip ran out and then he calmly set the gun down and walked to the edge of the roof and stood quiet just long enough for the ringing to dissipate and then he balled his fists and screamed.

Stage three, clearly singing now: *"I look like I been balling 'cause I'm really balling..."* Legs dangling from the edge of the roof, the soles of his shoes just inches above the water. *"I won't apologize, I'm not really sorry..."* Pistol in his hands, hands in his lap, eyes on the pistol. *"They ask me if I'm lying, I say, really really... I'm really out my mind, I say, really really."*

I daydreamed of walking off the edge of the roof and sinking into the murk. Rain and gator piss filling my lungs. It wouldn't even be a thing, I felt like, I'd just be whatever about it.

I got to thinking about our ghost, and if ghosts could swim, and if not, could they drown? I get that there's all those sea legends of sirens coaxing horny sailors to their doom, and yeah, I've seen *The Fog*, but we're talking about a house ghost. You have to figure ghosts aren't great at adapting if they can't even accept being dead. There was the two of us on the roof and the open air and the mosquitoes swarming above the water and none of it felt haunted. And that made me feel kinda hollow, mournful. So I dusted off the Ouija board we used as a rolling tray and I tried to concentrate. I asked our ghost if it was still with us, and was it okay. I had both hands on the planchette. I waited for it to move.

Catfish leapt out of the water in the yard. Marcel hummed a tune I knew but couldn't place. I didn't ask what it was because I didn't want him to stop. So I mimicked his humming, and finally it clicked, and with a grin, I sang, *"Twenty-five lighters on my dressuh, yessuh,"* and Marcel jumped to his feet and aimed his chest at the sky—every vein in his face popping out.

"I GOTS TO GET PAID!"

We went on and on like that, jumping around the roof singing Lil Keke while the fish flopped nearby.

"Twenty-five lighters on my dressuh, yessuh."

"I GOTS TO GET PAID!"

We broke one of the commandments and dipped into the bag. Marcel handed me a tablet shaped like Bart Simpson and I dry-swallowed and after a few minutes, my butthole felt really warm.

"I think I'm going to shit myself," I said.

Marcel was just like, "Haha, yeah."

I sort of bounced in place.

Marcel connected his phone to a pill-shaped speaker. Played Freddie Gibbs.

"Won't that drain the battery?" I said.

"It's going to die soon anyways," he said, "might as well go out with some music."

The bass vibrated through the soles of my feet all the way up to my face. I could feel my teeth rattling and just knew that if the top row touched the bottom row, all of my teeth would shatter, so I danced around the roof with my mouth wide open, trying not to shit my pants but also vibing to the music, enjoying the color of the dusty orange sky, and for a little while, this underwater world seemed beautiful.

Marcel's phone rang. Unsaved number from Phoenix. He swiped to answer. "I'm at three percent. What's up?"

The caller said, "Take me off speaker."

Marcel said, "Ain't nobody listening."

I kept my mouth shut.

Dude's voice sounded like he was talking through clenched teeth, but not like he was angry. More like his jaw was wired shut. "Got a job if you want it. Big payout. All you gotta do is drive."

"Say less. When you need it done?"

"You can get here tomorrow if you leave now. You'll take a car hauler up to Canada. Everything straight with your passport?"

Marcel frowned.

Phoenix said, "You still there? I can get someone else, just thought you'd want in on some easy mon—"

The phone died and Marcel chunked it hard. It did several flips in the air before splashing down in the murky water.

Marcel was quiet for a long time.

"Maybe it's for the best," I said. "Sounded like some sketch shit."

He picked at the skin around his thumb nail. He said, "Maybe we should visit her after this."

"Who, Grams?"

"Renée."

I said, "I'd make that drive with you."

He said, "That's a bet."

The sky turned the color of mud. We lay on our backs, sweating out the X in our systems. Marcel got to talking about aliens. He said the meteor that wiped out the dinosaurs was actually a chunk of this planet that was once between Mars and Jupiter. "There's a cluster of millions of asteroids still floating there," he said, "look it up. That's where our ancestors come from." I was still rolling like a motherfucker. Could feel my pulse in my eyeballs. Marcel sat up and wrapped his arms around his knees. "Think about it," he said. "We've been part of a world that's mostly water for how long now and we ain't seen but five percent of the ocean, yet we always blasting shit into outer space. We're homesick." Marcel rocked back and forth on his ass, knees against his chest. "Deep down," he said, "we know we don't belong here."

We were still rolling when we saw the horse walking on water. Radiuses of ripples spreading out from his hooves. Belly black with rot. He walked right along the roof's edge without stopping or paying any mind to us. I thought maybe we could hop on his back, catch a ride out, but Marcel didn't think so. "Probably shouldn't ride a dead horse," he said. "No telling where you'll end up."

We shared a can of cold chicken noodle. Marcel talked about windows between parallel worlds. "That's where Bigfoot and all of them come from," he said. "Flying saucers, chupacabra, all that shit. That's why we only ever catch glimpses. The windows don't stay open for long." I stared at the carrot chunk on my spoon. The dripping broth. Out of habit, I blew on it before taking a bite.

A drone flew across the high noon sky, casting the smallest shadow over the wet wreckage it was recording. Marcel hopped up and grabbed the carbine from one of the duffel bags. Shouldered it and followed the drone down the sights. Squeezed the trigger. The boom from the rifle muted the plastic explosion. The thing fell apart and rained down in pieces.

I said, "What'd you do that for?"

He said, "The tracking device. Whoever was controlling it is probably too close to be outside the flood zone, meaning they're in a boat. They see the drone go down, they'll head in the direction it dropped, and they'll find us and be heroes."

Another night came and went and there were no heroes. Marcel did pushups, bare hands pressed against the hot shingles. I was doubled over, dry-heaving at the edge of the roof, where the murky water had risen above the A/C unit in my bedroom window.

"Few years back," Marcel said, "there was this photo making rounds on the internet of this tiny-ass rock spewing out biomatter, like an interstellar nut sack blowing its load." A puddle of sweat formed below his face. He'd done at least a hundred pushups already. Sharp breaths between his words. "Could be how our DNA spread through the ocean. Body-snatching sea creatures. The genesis of our evolution."

I spit bile into the water and collapsed on my back and felt the warmth of the sun behind the orange clouds. I said, "You okay, man?"

Marcel stood over me. Tilted his head. "Am I okay?" He flexed his biceps, said, "Nigga, I'm out here getting swole." He did body builder poses. Pointed at me, still flexing. "You the one withering away with your pale, sickly ass."

I wanted him to know he wasn't alone in this. The universe had hit the reset button on us both. If we survived long enough to see dry land again, I'd be there for him. He was my best friend. But my mouth was dry and it hurt to say anything, so I just said, "You right."

Marcel said, "I'ma always be straight." He paced the roof, pausing every now and then to flex for nobody. "In the worst of times," he said, "dope sells itself." He gripped the duffel bag, raised it over his head. "And I've got that dope, *boyyy*! I'm muhfuckin Scarface!"

Boss Man the schizo vagrant floated by on an air mattress. He was shirtless beneath his tweed suit jacket and he was sipping on a tall boy. He raised his beer to us. Smile full of crooked yellow teeth. We saluted Boss Man as he floated down the street. He killed the beer and crushed the can against his head and tossed it in the water. Shouted something in drunk gibberish, skinny arms stretched high above his head. The king of the world.

At night, a single orb of light drifted across the sky, blinking in and out behind black clouds. I shook Marcel awake.

"We're getting out of here," I said, pointing to the sky. "Look." I pulled the Draco out of the gun bag and emptied the clip into the clouds and screamed until my chest got tight.

Marcel rubbed his eyes, said, "They're too far away." He rolled over and covered his face.

But he was wrong. The orb fell closer and closer until it hit the water and split into four more orbs, spread out in a diamond formation, glowing bright above the floating trash and belly-up catfish. The orbs spun, trading positions, tethered together by luminous tracers. A red triangle appeared in the center of the orbs and then all at once, whatever it was shot back up into the sky and we were alone again.

We recognized him right away by that half-shredded ear. He paddled his way toward us, head dipping under a couple times along the way. Marcel pressed his tongue against his teeth and shook his head. The coon pawed his way up to the roof, which wasn't much of a reach anymore. He shook the water from his fur and stood on his hind legs. Chest full of holes, raw meat pink and glistening. Marcel reached in the bag for what I guessed was a gun, and judging by that tattered ear twitching, the coon must have been guessing the same, maybe even hoping for it. Because maybe this next shot would be the one to end it. But Marcel only pulled out a Pop Tart. Opened the foil with his teeth and held the strawberry pastry at arm's length. He and the coon stared at each other for a good minute. Then the coon got on all fours and crawled slowly towards the sugary peace offering. Snatched it and wolfed it down. Crumbs in his whiskers. Marcel nodded at the coon and the coon scurried over to the duffel bag full of dope and sniffed at it. We both laughed. Marcel said, "You tryna get high, little nigga?" The coon hooked his head under the strap and took off to the edge of the roof, duffel dragging behind him. He leapt into the water and sank under the weight of the bag. Marcel said, "The fuck," and dove in after the coon. The waves and ripples settled. I crawled to the edge, seeing only my own distorted reflection in the clay-colored flood water. A few seconds later, Marcel's head broke through the surface. Eyes clenched, teeth bared. He used one arm to swim toward the roof. He gripped my wrist. I pulled him up. "I got it," he said, laughing. Cradled in his other arm was the coon, drenched fur spiked and dripping. They collapsed side by side on the shingles, Marcel still laughing, the coon's eyes closed. "I think he's dead," I said. Marcel raised an eyebrow. "Just give him a minute," he said. And he was right. Eventually, the coon wheezed and coughed and blinked his eyes open. Staggered up onto his hind legs. Shook the water from his fur. The three of us sat at the edge of the roof, unsure of what would come of us, or what to do with ourselves in the meantime. I had a few more ecstasy pills in my pocket.

Time was no longer a construct in the new world of rooftop islands. We'd been stranded for a week, maybe, but it could have been a month, could have been a few hours. The sky was the color of codeine and then it was black. When I slept—meaning, when I was fucked up enough to handle the sticky heat and the stench of underwater roadkill—I dreamed of the ruins of ancient planets floating around in outer space. Homesick as a bitch. We popped the last of the X and sang the songs we could remember all the words to and mumbled the rest. The coon would never look at us straight; always with that furry, scarred-up head tilted to one side. Those large, exasperated eyes. We tried catching fish with pastry crumbs tied to shoestrings, but never had any luck with it. If the snacks ran out before a boat came our way, we'd see how far out we could swim before a current or a gator pulled us under. Could have been we were already dead, trapped in some kind of flooded purgatory. The mosquitoes had moved on from us. I guess they don't bite dead things.

EDEN'S BASTARDS

We walked with our backs to the smoke and flames of the city. I squeezed my skull between my palms and went *grrr* and you pinched a little chunk of cartilage inside my ear, said if I pierced it, the migraines would go away.

I said, "You're kidding."

You said, "Swear."

"If it doesn't work," I said, "I'm hacking my fucking ears off."

We passed this building with busted-out windows and you knelt and plucked a shard of glass from the dirt and handed it to me, said, "Okay, deal."

I slid the glass inside my pocket.

In the distance, a banshee screamed. Inside my head, it echoed.

We walked under a ladder that was propped up against a concrete wall. The wall stood alone, severed from everything that once gave it purpose, rebar jutting out like exposed tendons.

We crossed the bridge where you said not to look over and I said I wouldn't, but I did, and there were a dozen bodies floating on their backs and I followed their lifeless gazes to the sky, where they last searched for god in the clouds, but saw only smoke.

You walked ahead down the river bank, watching your steps, checking back every few seconds to be sure I was close behind. Your black hair was glowing from the fire. I caught you sticking your tongue out to catch a flake of ash on your tongue and you looked back and smiled and I smiled back and we went on smiling, looking for sharp objects in the dark.

We came upon a grey body that'd been coughed up on the shore. You stopped inches from it and held up a hand.

"Hey, this oughtta work," you said, and then you planted your foot on the spine of the naked body and pulled an arrow out of its head. It made a wet, crunching sound as you twisted and yanked the thing out. Other arrows riddled the body's torso and legs, but we only needed one. You stuck the head of the arrow in the gentle flow of the river and then wiped it on your sleeve.

You stood next to me and said, "Tilt your head," and I did, and you closed one eye and squinted the other, two fingers pressed near the arrow head. You said, "Okay, ready?" but didn't wait for an answer. You stabbed the arrow through the little cartilage in my ear and it sounded like someone chewing on gravel and the pain was like a fire. You pushed it in until the edges of the arrowhead began to flare out and then you snapped off the wooden part of the arrow and left the sharp triangle stone in my ear.

I touched it and winced.

You kissed my ear and your lips were red.

My head swam, numb. I said, "I think it's working."

You smirked and gave a shrug like, *duh*. Your eyes fell to the face of the body beneath your shoe. You squinted, focusing a minute. Said, "Sort of looks like you."

I got on all fours next to the body's face and ran my fingers over the curvature of his cheekbones, down his nose and lips, caught my reflection in his black eyes. "Maybe this is my father," I said.

You said, "Yeah, could be," then skipped ahead with a lost interest.

I said to the body, "Sorry, dad," unsure of what my apology meant, just feeling like there were a lot of things to be sorry about. I got up and brushed myself off and called for you to wait up.

When I caught up to you, you slipped your fingers between mine and we walked on a little further until we came to the orchard graveyard, which is just something we named this vacant lot covered in building rubble and yellow grass and dead trees.

Somewhere in the distance, we heard a sick moaning that was more like hopeless hunger than passionate pleasure—a noise that was all too familiar around these parts. There were multiple voices belonging to some back-alley train of thrusting bodies that fucked mechanically with blank faces. We tuned them out, climbed to the top of a pile of debris and leaned against each other. From here, we could see the river carrying corpses, the field of dead trees, and the flames of the city licking the sky.

I asked if you thought things used to be different and you said, "It's always been this way, far as we know. What's it matter?" Then you touched the tip of the arrow sticking out of my ear and grinned, said, "It looks kinda cool."

I said, "Really?"

You curled your lip. "Sort of." Laid your head on my shoulder.

The bodies in the river rose and dipped and spun in circles. They were one with the waves. I think I might have seen a star through the smoke in the air.

ABOUT THE AUTHOR

KELBY LOSACK is a hoodrat noir and gutter cyberpunk author. He is co-host of the cult hit podcast Agitator with J David Osborne. Currently working on another novel, several screenplays, children's books, and short films. His last warrant was dropped in 2020. He lives with his wife and their two sons in Gulf Coast Texas, where he's tryna get the bag honestly and stay out the streets.

www.kelbylosack.com

ACKNOWLEDGEMENTS

Shouts out to the Broken River crew for the juice to keep going in harder—JDO, Eddy, Simmons, Grant, Rios—you're my family. To Mom and Dad for doing the opposite of most parents and encouraging their kid to make art. To the whole fam. To my kids, you blow my mind, each of you. Phoenix, the new joints were written almost exclusively at 3am when you were teething and fussing and I was too awake to go back to sleep so figured, *might as well write*, so thanks for that, buddy. To Brian Allen Carr, my brother. To Isaac, I miss you, dawg. To those who've dug my shit and helped push it from the jump. Robert Dean, John Wayne Comunale, Elle Nash, Max Booth III, Lori Michelle, Tobias Carroll, Michael Kazepis, Andrew Robertson, David James Keaton, Jedidiah Ayres, Scott Adlerberg, Jordan Harper, Justin Carter, Josh Jabcuga, Lucas Mangum, Tomasz Gałązka, Chris Kelso, Anthony Neil Smith, Brian Evenson, Matt Neil Hill, Benoit Lelievre, Francois Pointeau, Max Thrax, Jacob Everett, Tiffany Scandal, D'urban Moffer. To Marcus for those long, harsh hours entrenched in the bullshit—I learned more about writing through entertaining each other in various gutters than anywhere else, probably. To Luis Galindo, Courtney Lomelo, Reverend Janglebones, Kurt Huggins, Wren Collier, Mason, Nate aka Postmugglism—for all your wisdom and the shared magic. To the artists making up the soundtrack to late nights writing: Hogg Booma, Lunv D, Keenan Maxie, That Mexican OT, Z-Ro, Infennity, Sleep Token, Big Tony, Paul Wall, Devin the Dude, DJ Screw, Low Roar, Sigh, Cataplexy, Salem, Kanye West, Dirtyphonics, Skrillex, P.T. Adamczyk, White Ring, IC3PEAK, Yves V, Lorn, Getter, Health. To Mike Pondsmith and Hideo Kojima. To Kentaro Miura for *Berserk*, Tsutomu Nihei for *BLAME!*, and Takashi Miike for everything. To the raccoon with the golden disc, and that feral child writing on the walls. To Glen Rockney, Psi, Adam Lehrer, Will Samson, Jack Mason, Ryan Simón, Ryan Jackson, LowRes Wunderbread, Hans Lam Barboza, Zach Langley Chi-Chi, Sam aka Fella, Barrett Avner, Matthew Sini, Gordon White, Brendan. To the dog... I'm so sorry. To all the barrels I've stared down. To the people fishing off the jetties down at Surfside, and all the things you leave behind on the rocks. Gotta give flowers to those whose style and flow I've lifted elements from in the process of whipping up my own—Danny Brown, Lil Wayne, Irvine Welsh, Earl Sweatshirt, Stephen Graham Jones, Chuck Palahniuk, Jeremy Robert Johnson, Drakeo the Ruler, Chester

Watson, Cody Goodfellow, Bret Easton Ellis, all the folks from the stoop to the pulpit whose rhythms of speech play on a loop in my subconscious. To myself. To those I hope aren't reading this, will never ever find this, but if you did find it and read up to a certain point and trashed the book and cursed my name—my bad, I guess, but not really. To Jay Springett, Alex Kazemi, Nick and Jayson and all the Agitator patrons, Lily and Mason and Brandon and those already mentioned from the workshop, G.D. Bowlin, Tom Wickersham, Jim Ruland, Kris Saknussemm, Sean Kilpatrick, Sam Pink, Kyle Muntz, Manuel Merrero, Bud Smith, Calvin Westra, Evan Dean Shelton, Bobby LaFollette, DuVay Knox, Kevin Maloney, Justin Lutz, James McNally, Troy James Weaver. To A.A. Medina for this dope cover. And more than anything, deepest thanks, and many apologies, to Erika—my love, my light, my ride-or-die—for continuing to thug it out with me. We're going to make it out on top, babe.

New from Broken River

Rock City

by G.D. Bowlin

An Altar of Stories to Liminal Saints

by Rios de la Luz

Melancholy's Finest: The Motorpapi Chronicles, Book 1

by Grant Wamack

The Howling Earth: Iron Wolf

by E Rathke

Ghosts of West Baltimore

by David Simmons

Gods Fare No Better: A War In Heaven

by J. David Osborne

The Howling Earth: Broken Katana

by E Rathke

Noir: A Love Story

by E Rathke

Bullet Tooth

by Grant Wamack

brokenriverbooks.com

Made in the USA
Middletown, DE
19 March 2024

51273575R00099